A ROAD TO ROMANCE

Then on a straight stretch, where he could see for nearly half a mile, he became aware that there was a horse behind him. The Marquis was not riding at a particularly fast pace at that stage and a moment or so later the horse drew level with him.

He turned his head to see a young girl riding what he recognised at once was a well bred horse.

She was close beside him and he looked at her in some surprise, thinking that there was plenty of room on the empty road for both of them.

Then she spoke in a hesitating and shy voice,

"Would you mind – very much, sir, if I rode beside – you?"

The Marquis looked at her again.

"Is there any reason why you should ask that?" he enquired.

She looked over her shoulder in an anxious way.

"It seems as if you are running away," the Marquis then remarked.

"That is exactly – what I am doing," she replied, "and it will help me considerably – if I can ride with you up this long straight road."

The Marquis was curious and then he said,

"I do not wish to seem impertinent, but I would like to know why."

"I will tell you if we can – go a little faster," the girl answered him nervously.

THE BARBARA CARTLAND PINK COLLECTION

Titles in this series

A ROAD TO ROMANCE

BARBARA CARTLAND

Barbaracartland.com Ltd

THE BARBARA CARTLAND PINK COLLECTION

Dame Barbara Cartland is still regarded as the most prolific bestselling author in the history of the world.

In her lifetime she was frequently in the Guinness Book of Records for writing more books than any other living author.

Her most amazing literary feat was to double her output from 10 books a year to over 20 books a year when she was 77 to meet the huge demand.

She went on writing continuously at this rate for 20 years and wrote her very last book at the age of 97, thus completing an incredible 400 books between the ages of 77 and 97.

Her publishers finally could not keep up with this phenomenal output, so at her death in 2000 she left behind an amazing 160 unpublished manuscripts, something that no other author has ever achieved.

Barbara's son, Ian McCorquodale, together with his daughter Iona, felt that it was their sacred duty to publish all these titles for Barbara's millions of admirers all over the world who so love her wonderful romances.

So in 2004 they started publishing the 160 brand new Barbara Cartlands as *The Barbara Cartland Pink Collection*, as Barbara's favourite colour was always pink – and yet more pink!

The Barbara Cartland Pink Collection is published monthly exclusively by Barbaracartland.com and the books are numbered in sequence from 1 to 160.

Enjoy receiving a brand new Barbara Cartland book each month by taking out an annual subscription to the Pink Collection, or purchase the books individually.

The Pink Collection is available from the Barbara Cartland website www.barbaracartland.com via mail order and through all good bookshops.

In addition Ian and Iona are proud to announce that The Barbara Cartland Pink Collection is now available in ebook format as from Valentine's Day 2011.

For more information, please contact us at:

Barbaracartland.com Ltd.
Camfield Place
Hatfield
Hertfordshire AL9 6JE
United Kingdom

Telephone: +44 (0)1707 642629
Fax: +44 (0)1707 663041
Email: info@barbaracartland.com

THE LATE DAME BARBARA CARTLAND

Barbara Cartland who sadly died in May 2000 at the age of nearly 99 was the world's most famous romantic novelist who wrote 723 books in her lifetime with worldwide sales of over 1 billion copies and her books were translated into 36 different languages.

As well as romantic novels, she wrote historical biographies, 6 autobiographies, theatrical plays, books of advice on life, love, vitamins and cookery. She also found time to be a political speaker and television and radio personality.

She wrote her first book at the age of 21 and this was called *Jigsaw*. It became an immediate bestseller and sold 100,000 copies in hardback and was translated into 6 different languages. She wrote continuously throughout her life, writing bestsellers for an astonishing 76 years. Her books have always been immensely popular in the United States, where in 1976 her current books were at numbers 1 & 2 in the B. Dalton bestsellers list, a feat never achieved before or since by any author.

Barbara Cartland became a legend in her own lifetime and will be best remembered for her wonderful romantic novels, so loved by her millions of readers throughout the world.

Her books will always be treasured for their moral message, her pure and innocent heroines, her good looking and dashing heroes and above all her belief that the power of love is more important than anything else in everyone's life.

"A road to anywhere new and exciting can often seem like a challenge too far. In my life I have always believed that one should try out new ideas, new places and new destinations. Something positive will always follow and who knows romance may not be very far behind."

Barbara Cartland

CHAPTER ONE
1820

The Marquis of Whisinford turned into St. James's Street and walked into White's Club.

Having nodded to the porter, he then went into the coffee room.

As expected, he saw his friend, who he was having luncheon with, waiting for him.

Lord Alfred Middleton and the Marquis had been at Eton and Oxford together.

They were now enjoying the London Season and met almost every night at some party or other.

Last night the Marquis had been dancing with an extremely pretty girl who Lord Alfred had not seen before.

So he greeted his friend when he joined him saying,

"Did she or did she not?"

"She did not purely because I did not ask her," the Marquis replied and they both laughed.

The Marquis ordered some coffee and Lord Alfred raised his eyebrows.

"Since when," he asked "have you been drinking coffee before luncheon?"

"As a matter of fact I did not think the champagne last night was particularly good," the Marquis replied, "and the port they provided, I am certain was corked."

"I never touch port," Lord Alfred said, "so I don't know."

"I don't often either, but I was really rather bored."

Lord Alfred sighed.

"I can understand that. We have been to at least ten parties that were exactly the same as the one last night with more or less the same people, but I thought that the woman you were dancing with was superior to the others."

"She is married to a diplomat and therefore has a French *chic* about her because they are habitually in Paris," the Marquis answered. "At the same time she made it very clear to me that she was never unfaithful to her husband!"

Lord Alfred laughed.

"So a wasted evening."

"It was not just a waste from that point of view, but altogether the Season is becoming duller and duller. Or perhaps it's because we are getting older and older."

"I think that is the real reason," Lord Alfred agreed. "We are nearing twenty-six and as you know most of the young gentlemen enjoying themselves last night had only just left Oxford and had not reached their twenty-second or twenty-third birthday."

He paused and the Marquis interrupted,

"In another few years they too will be like us, bored with doing the same thing over and over again."

As he was speaking with undisguised vehemence, Lord Alfred stared at him.

"Is it really as bad as all that?" he asked.

"Well, ask yourself, Alfred, I must say I have found not only the *Beau Monde* a bore, but also the pretty 'soiled doves' are not as amusing as I used to think they were."

Lord Alfred sighed.

He knew the Marquis was referring to the 'Houses of Pleasure' which were situated around St. James's Street. It was where they often went when they were bored with the Social world and they usually found a number of their friends doing the same thing.

There was silence for a moment,

Then the Marquis quizzed his friend,

"What can we do, Alfred, which is new and original and where can we find someone attractive to do it with us?"

Lord Alfred laughed.

"You can hardly take a 'soiled dove' with you to a private ball or for that matter anywhere except where they officially belong."

"I know! I know!" the Marquis groaned. "But you do see that we are caught in a cage that we cannot possibly escape from."

"What do you mean by that?" Lord Alfred asked.

"Well, the first thing is we are matrimonial catches and are watched by every ambitious Mama as well as the *debutantes* of the year themselves."

"I am well aware of that, Neil, but I can assure you that I avoid that sort of *debutante*. I was so nearly caught the first year after I left Oxford."

The Marquis nodded.

"As you can imagine I was walking with caution even then. I was very nearly trapped not once but several times."

"I remember that," Lord Alfred said. "You almost had to marry the Heathcote girl. There were even bets here at White's that you would be married before the year was out."

"We have both been very clever. We have avoided the more obvious traps. At the same time I am beginning to become extremely bored!"

"Do you really mean that?" Lord Alfred asked.

There was a pause before the Marquis said,

"I suppose that we could go round the world, but it would be much the same when we came back. I have now become extremely suspicious of every invitation I receive, even when it is for riding or shooting."

"Now you are exaggerating, Neil. Equally I know of certain houses where I am invited every year."

"Me too," the Marquis said.

"Although the shooting is good and I much enjoy being there," Lord Alfred continued, "I am always terrified in case I should come back with a chain round my legs and a wedding ring looming over my head!"

The Marquis chuckled.

"You are becoming quite lyrical about it. What we really ought to do is to write a book revealing how difficult it is to escape all the ambitious mothers and the girls who cling to us like scorpions."

"Do you really think it could be a guide for every young gentleman who follows us?" Lord Alfred asked.

"I think they would agree that every word we have written is the truth," the Marquis replied. "At the same time we would be barred from the Social world and have nothing to do except for joining the little blossoms who are waiting for us eagerly at the 'Temples of Joy'."

Lord Alfred laughed.

"That is a new name for them."

"Oh, they have often used it before. In fact they have used every word to entice us in and I am sick to death of being enticed!"

"Rubbish," Lord Alfred replied. "You enjoy it, you know you do! You are handsome, you are rich and have a good title and some outstanding racehorses."

"They at least are my consolation and I am never bored with them any more than you become bored with yours. By the way, Alfred, are you entering the Doncaster races this year?"

"I hope so," he replied. "My trainer would be livid if I did not enter for at least two races."

"I am thinking of doing the same. Perhaps in the North we will find it more amusing than it is here."

"I don't know what's the matter with you, Neil. I have never known you so depressed and against the Social world, as they call it, as you are now."

There was a moment of silence and then he asked,

"Is it possible you have been crossed in love?"

The Marquis laughed again.

"Trust you to think of that, Alfred! No I have not been crossed! In fact I am over-encouraged if that is the right word for it. I am not quite certain how to break off my present *affaire-de-coeur* without creating a scene."

Lord Alfred groaned.

"Oh, those scenes, how ghastly they are! 'Why do you not love me now? Why are you suddenly different? Who can be standing between us?' I have heard them all a thousand times."

"So have I, even if you do exaggerate the numbers slightly, Alfred. I do think that you were rather foolish to leave the last beauty. After all her husband is permanently fishing or shooting somewhere and so you don't have to be nervous every time a door creaks."

Lord Alfred smiled.

"I think that has happened to all of us at one time. But perhaps we have grown not only older and wiser but older and more careful."

"I am not worrying myself about being careful," the Marquis replied. "But how to leave the stage, so to speak, with dignity and without a scene, tears, protestations and occasionally unbridled anger."

"I know it only too well. Now you are free and I am in the same position, what shall we do about it?" Lord Alfred questioned.

"What can we do? Except go hunting for more and meet here in a couple of months' time to say exactly the same things to each other that we have said now."

Lord Alfred held up his hands.

"What you want now is a good drink of champagne which I will stand you. Let's decide to go somewhere new where we have never been before and see if the women are more attractive than those we find in London."

"If you are talking of leaving England, Alfred, you know as well as I do that we have to be here because of all the racing. Otherwise it's not a bad idea and we certainly might do it in the autumn."

There was silence as they sipped their coffee.

Then Lord Alfred remarked,

"Well, the autumn is very far away. Let's think of something exciting. Something we have never done before which we can do at once when you are down in the dumps. As I have already told you I am, at the moment, open to any offers made to me."

"They will be made all right," the Marquis said in a gloomy voice. "Just as I know that Beaufort is determined that I will marry his daughter."

Lord Alfred gave a cry.

"Oh, you cannot do that! She is a crashing bore! He tried to push her onto me for some time and I was fool enough to enjoy his food, his drink and the amusing people he entertained and was then very nearly forced up the aisle because of it."

"I have been in exactly the same position too," the Marquis murmured. "It's those people we must avoid at all costs."

Lord Alfred then called the Steward and ordered a bottle of champagne.

"Now I am determined to cheer you up, Neil," he said, "and you will find that champagne is always helpful on these occasions."

"I have a better idea," a voice rang out.

Both of them turned to look at the speaker.

It was the Duke of Dunstead, who had been sitting behind them although they had not been aware of it.

He was an old man and one of the most respected members of White's.

He walked round the Marquis's chair and sat down between them.

"I have been listening to what you were saying," he said. "I found it amusing, because I went through exactly the same troubles myself when I was your age."

"I am sure you did," Lord Alfred agreed. "After all, you became a Duke and I am certain that all the young *debutantes* dream that a Duke will fall down the chimney and ask her to marry him. Then, as a Duchess, she will be one of the most important people in the whole of Society."

The Duke laughed.

"That is more or less true," he said. "You are both going through what I went through a thousand times and thought I was unique, just as you think you are."

"We don't think that we are unique," the Marquis argued. "But you must admit that the Social world, Your

Grace, can be extremely boring or perhaps it was better in your day."

"Only if it becomes, as you yourselves have found it, repetitive," the Duke replied. "And that I understand is the reason why both of you are up in arms."

"I only wish we were," Lord Alfred said. "And Neil is particularly fed up at the moment simply because they run after him too readily. Instead of enjoying himself as he ought to, he is more intent on not being caught."

The Duke smiled.

"A sad, sad story! Well then, I have something to suggest to you two boys that I really wish someone had suggested to me."

"What is that?" the Marquis asked, now looking interested.

"What I wanted and what you need at the moment is adventure," he replied. "I don't mean going out and exploring the world outside but seeing if there is adventure, which, of course, there is in our own country."

Both young gentlemen stared at him.

"You said 'adventure'," the Marquis queried.

"That is just what I mean," the Duke said. "I have always believed it is to be found here at home if one looks for it or is fortunate enough to fall into it by the wayside."

Lord Alfred was looking at him with surprise.

"Then are you really suggesting, Your Grace, that in your long and exciting life you have found adventure here in England?"

"Yes, that is just what I am saying, my boy. As you know, I have fought abroad in the Army. I have been involved in many skirmishes and have travelled to strange places that I found very interesting if uncomfortable."

The Marquis laughed.

"I would have thought that the adventures you had which, when they were happening, must have been most unpleasant for the body besides being somewhat explosive to the brain."

"You are absolutely right," the Duke agreed. "But I have thought, as I am thinking now, that adventure is here for all of us if we are fortunate enough to find it."

"You mean here in England," Lord Alfred asked, as if he must get it straight in his own mind.

"Exactly! I am therefore going to suggest, although you may refuse, thinking I am a stupid old man to propose it or you may well think it is a new idea and something that you have never done before."

Both the Marquis and Lord Alfred sat forward in their seats with their eyes on the Duke.

He could see that they were listening.

"Because in White's we have to put it down in the betting book," he said, "I am prepared to bet you one of my best horses to one of yours that if you set out alone from here in London to, shall we say, the North of England or Land's End, you will both find adventure you had never thought of before and certainly have never encountered."

They were silent for a moment.

Then the Marquis said,

"I cannot imagine what it could be unless we were held up by a highwayman or two."

"You could certainly do that but that is not what I am thinking of."

"Explain it to us," Lord Alfred begged him.

"Well, I am quite certain that for every man there comes a moment in his life when he encounters difficulties and problems either physically or mentally that require all his intelligence and all his training to solve. You have both been extremely well educated and you have also seen the Social world at its best – and its worst."

The Duke paused before he went on,

"I would like to think that if you went out alone, incognito, you would encounter a very different world to the one you know already. After all you have both come from famous families and you both hold titles which are respected and envied."

He smiled as he went on,

"It would be good for you to see your own country in an entirely different way from how you view it at the moment."

They looked at him in astonishment.

Then Lord Alfred enquired,

"What exactly is Your Grace suggesting we do?"

"As I have already said, I am making a bet of it. I will bet one of my best horses and you know that my stable is one of the best, if you win. But if you lose then I have the pick of one of yours."

Lord Alfred laughed.

"That is certainly a magnificent bet and a similar one I feel sure is not in the betting book."

"No, I don't think that it will be," the Duke agreed. "But it means if you accept my bet that you set off one of you going North and the other one going South and return when you reach the end of your journey."

The two of them gazed at each other in amazement.

"If I lose my bet," the Duke carried on, "then my stable is at your disposal, otherwise you give me a choice of all your racehorses, several of which I admit that I have envied for some time."

The Marquis grinned.

"It's a good way for Your Grace to acquire them."

"Exactly. Of course you can easily turn down my suggestion. But I think if you are as adventurous as you sound and as adventurous as I was in my youth, you will find that it gives you a new outlook, a new knowledge of people and above all a new interest which is something you apparently find lacking in your lives at this moment."

"That's true!" Lord Alfred exclaimed. "As I expect Your Grace heard us saying, we are bored. Both of us at present have no particular female interest that will prevent us from accepting your very unusual and original bet."

"Do you really think," the Marquis asked, "that we would find anything outstandingly different or particularly interesting on our long ride."

"I am quite certain you will," the Duke answered. "I think, too, it will be good for both of you to become one of the ordinary people, which means, of course, that you must disguise yourself as ordinary Englishmen."

"I am glad that we will at least be allowed to do that," Lord Alfred commented a little sarcastically.

"It would be difficult to disguise the fact that you are well-bred," the Duke replied seriously. "Therefore if you are just Mr. Smith or Mr. Jones, no one will question that you are anything else. Why should they?"

Unexpectedly the Marquis laughed.

"I can hardly believe it! I came to White's feeling depressed and, as Your Grace has heard, bored stiff with life that has become incredibly humdrum. The same thing happens day after day and the same applies to nights which are never quite as exciting as one expects them to be."

The Duke nodded.

"I know that, too. As you are both aware, but too polite to say so, there were a great number of women in my

11

life. In fact, as you know, I was called a roué before I was twenty-five!"

He paused for a moment and then added smiling,

"I don't regret any of it. Nor do I regret the times I have felt it wise to leave England because my reputation had become so outrageous that it rivalled that of the Prince Regent!"

Both of them laughed.

"It must have been most satisfactory in some way," Lord Alfred said.

"I suppose it was," the Duke replied. "But it must have meant a great deal of worry for my family. I freely admit now, that on many occasions, I left England simply because things had grown too hot for me here."

"At least then you were never bored," the Marquis remarked, "as we are at present."

"That is true, even though I was at times scared, although I would not admit it, at the chaos I had caused."

"And you think, Your Grace, that because we are bored and somewhat blasé," Lord Alfred said, "that we will find a cure for all our ills on the hard road."

"I will be very disappointed if you don't find a new interest and a new outlook. What we all need in our lives is variety and, of course, stimulation of the brain."

They looked at him in surprise.

They had somehow never expected the Duke, who, as he had said himself, was well known as a roué, to talk so seriously or in fact to be so concerned with them.

"Are you saying, Your Grace," the Marquis asked, "that you regret a great many things you did in your life?"

The Duke thought for a moment.

"I do not exactly regret them. But I often wonder if I had taken a different road or found a different solution it would have been better not only for me but for the people concerned."

"Well, one thing we cannot do is to put back the clock," Lord Alfred said. "I am sure, Your Grace, you do not regret the life you have led, which to us sounds a very exciting one. It would undoubtedly be better to have all the difficulties you have experienced rather than remain here feeling poor and getting nowhere."

"I agree with you completely," the Duke replied. "That is why I have made this suggestion, or rather this bet, and I do hope you will both take me up on it."

"I certainly will!" the Marquis said. "Even though I feel that Your Grace is wrong and all I will have is a lonely road North and nothing exciting will happen except as I have already suggested a highwayman will strip me of my money and my horse."

"Well, at least you can take a pistol with you to prevent that from happening," Lord Alfred remarked. "It is something I will do."

The Marquis laughed.

"I think maybe, Your Grace, you should come with me and protect me," he said.

The Duke put up his hand.

"Definitely no! My bet is that you should go alone. An adventure might not drop from the skies for two men together. But for one man alone, I am certain it will be lurking in every shadow."

"Now you are making me determined to prove you wrong," the Marquis parried. "After all, that is the whole point of a bet, is it not?"

"Of course it is," the Duke agreed. "And if you take my bet, Whisinford, I am quite certain that you will find it will help you in your future. Who knows you may find a new interest or a special happiness you have never known before."

"Now Your Grace is being really optimistic and I only hope you are right. When would you like us to start?"

"At the very latest, tomorrow! What is the point of staying here? You will go to a party tonight which you will find as boring as the party you attended last night. Or you will both be involved in a new *affaire-de-coeur* which instead of going to the country will keep you in London."

"He is quite right," Lord Alfred said to the Marquis. "You will remember that the party tonight is being given by the Countess of Coventry for her two extremely plain and unattractive daughters."

The Marquis groaned.

"I was, in point of fact, wondering how I could excuse myself at the last moment, but so far I had not come up with any reasonable excuse."

"Well, here is one that you cannot argue about," the Duke said. "You can write a polite letter to your hostess saying you have been called away on important business and just hope she will understand that in consequence, you cannot be present."

"What am I to say?" Lord Alfred then asked.

"I think your excuse should be that you have a very bad headache," he answered, "and feel that you would be poor company to anyone you danced with and might in fact be infectious."

Lord Alfred clapped and lay back in his chair.

"I am extremely grateful to Your Grace for saving me from a very dreary party and you must tell us what time you wish us to leave in the morning and from where?"

"I have thought of that already. You will come to my house in Berkeley Square at seven o'clock precisely where breakfast will be waiting for you. I would presume that both of you have horses stabled in London."

He paused before he added quickly,

"In fact I am sure you have, as both of you have runners at Henley on Thursday."

"You are right," the Marquis agreed. "I brought three horses up from the country just in case one was not up to scratch on the day of the races."

"Because Neil convinced me that was the best thing to do, I have done the same," Lord Alfred joined in.

"Very well! You will come to breakfast with me. Then your grooms will bring your horses to the Mews and so you will leave at eight o'clock exactly with Whisinford going North and you, Middleton, going South-West. The bet ends as soon as you have reached your destination and you will doubtless wish to return perhaps by sea or in a quicker and more comfortable manner."

It passed through the Marquis's mind that he had friends who lived just outside Northumberland who would undoubtedly loan him horses and a phaeton if he needed one to return home rapidly.

As if he knew what he was thinking, the Duke said, with a twinkle in his eye,

"Then, of course, you may want to stay longer than is necessary, so you should take enough money with you and a change of clothes which any good horse can carry as well as his Master."

"You think of everything!" Lord Alfred exclaimed. "Actually I am feeling extremely excited at your bet as it's something I have never done and, as you have doubtless heard me saying to Neil that we are not only bored with what is happening but becoming bores ourselves!"

The Duke smiled.

"I would think you have a few years of dissipation to enjoy before that happens. At the same time, as you well know, people who live in large houses with every possible comfort do become bores in their old age. It is, in fact, the adventures of life and the difficulties which make them not only human but also quite interesting."

"Like yourself." the Marquis proposed.

The Duke smiled again.

"Thanks for the compliment, my boy. At the same time it's true. I often think that, if I had been a good lad as I was expected to be until I took my father's place, I would not have lived as fully as I have."

He hesitated for a moment before he went on,

"Not that people have always approved of me, in fact, very much the opposite. Equally I have made a great number of good friends who, believe it or not, still find me somewhat amusing and interesting and who will then seek my company whenever I come to London and follow me when I go to the country."

"Of course they do," the Marquis agreed, "and we are flattered and, of course, intrigued by your interest in us. I only hope that we will not disappoint you and come back with nothing new to tell."

"I am betting there will be plenty," the Duke said. "It will give me a great deal of pleasure to feel that I have, at least, directed you onto a new road that you have never journeyed on before."

"That is indeed true," Lord Alfred said. "But now we have to think of what names we will call ourselves so that, if by any chance we need your help, you will not think it is from a stranger."

"I suggest you take very ordinary names so that you would not strike anyone as being particularly unusual."

There was silence while both of them thought.

Then the Marquis said,

"I had a teacher at Eton who I remember as being a very clever man. So I think I will call myself by his name. He is dead, so he will not mind my impersonating him."

"Which one are you talking about?" Lord Alfred asked.

"Barlow," the Marquis replied. "Do you remember Barlow? He coached us at cricket, amongst other things."

"Of course I remember him. So you will be Neil Barlow and then I will be Alfred Milton. Do you remember Milton?"

"Yes, indeed I do. We are setting out on a new and extraordinary adventure. Only I cannot help feeling that His Grace may be disappointed and we will return even more despondent than we are at the moment."

"It's a challenge which I have never had before and that alone makes it unique," Lord Alfred observed.

He raised his glass.

"To Your Grace, and may you never regret lifting us out of our gloom."

"I will drink to that," the Duke replied.

They raised their glasses.

When he had drunk his, the Duke rose to his feet.

"I am now going to luncheon," he said, "and I will look forward to seeing both of you tomorrow morning at seven o'clock in Berkeley Square."

He moved away before either of them could rise.

As they sank back in their chairs, Lord Alfred said,

"Well, it's certainly something new and there is one horse I would particularly like to own. I expect you know it, Neil, as it was a good winner at Cheltenham last week."

"I was thinking of that one myself," the Marquis replied. "Actually the Duke has a very fine collection and I would be delighted to include any of them with mine."

"As your stables and the Duke's are far larger than mine," Lord Alfred said, "I should be delighted for any contribution."

"I just cannot imagine what sort of adventures we are likely to have," the Marquis ruminated. "If you ask me we will come back with sad tales of losing our best horses, having our money pickpocketed or taken by highwaymen and the only women we are likely to talk to on the journey are the somewhat slovenly maids in the local inns where we will be staying."

Lord Alfred chuckled.

"That is very typical of you, Neil. You are always looking on the black side. Perhaps this journey will cheer you up and you will feel a different man after it."

"To be very frank with you I think that exceedingly unlikely. After all we both know that England is rather a dull country and the peasants are not particularly attractive, as you might find them in any foreign land."

He sipped a little more champagne and went on,

"If you ask me we will be spending nights in most uncomfortable circumstances. And we will eat food that is inedible and come home without anything happening that does not happen almost every day in the villages we own round our ancestral estates."

Lord Alfred threw up his hands.

"That is just the sort of thing you would say. Well, I am quite certain I will find excitement every mile and will return home to choose the Duke's best horse."

He laughed before he added.

"I will also find, as no man has found before, the most beautiful girl in the world!"

"Who will refuse you, because you are merely Mr. Milton and she will be looking for a Lord at least!"

Lord Alfred laughed and retorted,

"Poor Neil, if every man gets what he expects, that will be your lot! Whilst I will surely be finding adventures everywhere I stay and every day as I go to Land's End."

"Very well, Alfred, I will now bet you a thousand pounds that you have to admit when you get back it has been a waste of time and the country has provided you with nothing you have not had in abundance before."

"I will accept that bet," Lord Alfred replied. "We will write it down in the betting book."

"No, I will take your word as a gentleman and a member of White's Club not to cheat on it. But I think it would be a mistake for anyone to know what we are doing, in case it enters their heads to make a good story out of it that would make us the laughing stock of the Club."

"I see your point," Lord Alfred agreed, "and I will naturally accept your word of honour. Only there must be no cheating or in other words using your imagination."

"No, of course not," the Marquis replied. "I would not think of such a thing and if nothing else you will know the truth at the end of my journey."

"That is something to look forward to at any rate," the Marquis said brightly.

"So what are we going to do tonight?" Lord Alfred asked. "Our last night of freedom, so to speak."

"If we are determined not to go to tonight's party, we cannot be seen in public. Perhaps we are making fools of ourselves by accepting the Duke's bet."

"You are thinking that already?" he asked.

"Well, it's really rather a bore to have to ride all the way to the North alone. As I already suspect, there will be nothing better than bad food, bad beds and drab women!"

Lord Alfred grinned.

"I am expecting the very opposite. There will be excitement, amusement and a beautiful woman, an angel in disguise, who will invite me into her castle and I will then become, at first sight, infatuated by her."

The Marquis suppressed a laugh.

Then he said somewhat sourly,

"You will doubtless be able to write a book about that. But not a word of it will be true."

"No one knows. Unless you come back full of new ideas and new interests, I will marry you off to the most ambitious *debutante* of the year and you will settle down in the country for the rest of your life."

"Now that is a threat and not a promise. I will miss you, Alfred, while I am travelling alone. I think it rather unkind of the Duke to send you in the opposite direction."

"I must say I am surprised at the old boy coming up with something so original and in fact so intriguing," Lord Alfred said. "I really believe that it will be very good for both of us to experience the world from another aspect and not because we are both extremely eligible bachelors."

"I have often thought of wearing a notice saying 'not eligible' on the collar of my coat, so that I can show it to those young women who are thrust upon me by eager mothers determined that they should be my bride."

Lord Alfred looked at him curiously before he said,

"Have you ever been in love, Neil?"

"I thought I was once or twice, but it has always proved to be an illusion and sooner or later she has become a demanding and grasping dullard just like so many other women have been."

"You have been my best friend ever since we were at Eton," Lord Alfred said," but I have never known you so depressed, bitter, if that's the right word for it, and against the world, as you are at the moment."

"I think," the Marquis said slowly, "that it is either indigestion or the result of having too much too often. To be honest with you I am just sick to death of being chased. Not because I am an attractive man, but because I have an important title. I am tired of hearing the same reproaches and pleadings when one so-called love affair finishes."

"Well, all I can say," Lord Alfred said, "is that this is a case of kill or cure. You will either come back worse than you are at the moment or immensely better. I would not really like to bet on either."

"Keep your money in your pocket and, as we have no wish to be anywhere tonight, come and dine with me."

He paused before he added,

"At least we will eat a very good meal and enjoy some outstanding wines before we then set out on a trip in which we will have nothing but beer and sausages!"

Lord Alfred threw back his head and laughed.

Then he said,

"I am going home now to pack what I will need for tomorrow."

He drank down the last of his glass of champagne as he finished speaking.

Then he stood up and the Marquis did the same.

As they walked out of the morning room, they were both looking somewhat serious.

Two members, as they saw them pass by, wondered what could have happened to the two most handsome and debonair young gentlemen of White's Club.

CHAPTER TWO

The Marquis drove back to his house in Belgrave Square.

When he went upstairs to his bedroom, he found his valet waiting for him.

Herbert had been with him for years and he was the only one of his large staff he ever talked intimately to.

As he had said to one of his friends,

"No man is ever a hero to his valet. But a valet is unfortunately so much with one that it's impossible not to be confidential."

"And indiscreet," his friend added, laughing.

When the Marquis was in his large bedroom, which overlooked the square, he turned to Herbert and said,

"Herbert, I am taking part in a bet and I need your help."

"Not another one, my Lord!" Herbert exclaimed. "You know the last one was a disaster."

"I don't want to talk about it," the Marquis replied. "This is something new and which I am certain I will find extremely uncomfortable."

Herbert, who was over forty years of age, looked at him with a worried expression in his eyes.

He was really devoted to the young man he looked after and he was always frightened that he would become involved with some woman, who would be only marrying him for his title and his money and who would inevitably make him unhappy.

The Marquis took off his coat and threw it onto the chair.

"Now listen, Herbert! I have taken a bet that I will ride anonymously to the far North of England and not have any adventure or anything exciting to relate when I return."

Herbert was listening to his Lordship attentively and wondering exactly what this meant.

"If I do have an adventure, then I gain one of the horses I have always envied that belongs to the Duke of Dunstead."

Herbert smiled.

"His Grace has indeed an excellent stable. If your Lordship's allowed to choose, it'll be difficult because so many of them have been winners of the Classics."

"I know," the Marquis said, "and if I don't have any adventure worth reporting, then I have to give him one of my horses."

Herbert shook his head.

"You won't be able to deceive His Grace, my Lord, he'll take one of the very best."

"I am aware of that, Herbert. So I have to look out for an adventure, but goodness knows what I can expect if I am just Neil Barlow."

Herbert chuckled.

"You don't look like anyone called Barlow to me, my Lord!"

"Well, you will have to make me look ordinary or people will be too frightened to speak to me let alone ask my help in some disaster such as a pretty girl falling off a cliff or an even prettier one drowning in the river!"

"I'll be surprised if your Lordship has anything like that to cope with."

"Well, if I don't," the Marquis replied gloomily, "I will lose one of my best horses. And I cannot think of one I would ever like to part with."

He thought for a moment before he continued,

"Well, the dies are cast and you have to make me look like Barlow. I can only take clothes with me which I can carry on Samson's back."

"I guessed that it'd be Samson you'd choose to take with you," Herbert said. "He be a very fine horse. You be careful you don't lose him if you're goin' unprotected."

"I will take a pistol. Just a small one, which will go in my pocket, in case I encounter a highwayman."

"There's always a danger of that, my Lord. If you Lordship takes my advice, you'll keep to the main roads. It's going off on side tracks that gets one into trouble."

"I can see the sense of that," the Marquis remarked. "Now what I want you to do, Herbert, is to wait a week, then journey, if you like by sea, up to my cousin's castle in Northumberland."

"I remembers it although your Lordship's not been there in the last three years."

"Well, as I have to go to Northumberland, I might as well, when I arrive, be comfortable. I am sure that my cousin will be delighted to see me."

"That he will, my Lord, and if you asks me, you've rather neglected him these last years when you've been so wanted here in London."

The Marquis realised that he was referring to the enormous number of invitations he had had from what he and Alfred thought were ambitious mothers as well as the beautiful ladies he had enjoyed *affaires-de-coeur* with.

He had indeed stayed several times with his cousin, who had always been extremely kind to him when he was at Eton and Oxford and it was quite true to say that he had not been in touch for some time.

'So I will make it up to him now,' he thought to himself.

Then he said aloud to Herbert,

"You must take with you all the clothes I will need and, of course, a present to apologise for my recent neglect, if that is what you call it, these last three years."

"I knows what his Lordship really enjoys," Herbert said, "and you can leave it to me."

"I know I can, but, as you well know, I must have a change of shirts if nothing else and I cannot have dinner every night, wherever I am, in my riding breeches."

"Now you leave it to me, my Lord. I knows what Samson can carry and what he can't. What time will you be settin' off tomorrow mornin'?"

"I am meeting with Lord Alfred, who has accepted the same bet I have, who is going South to Cornwall, at the Duke of Dunstead's house at seven o'clock for breakfast."

"I thinks, my Lord," Herbert said after a moment's pause, "the earlier you go the less commotion it'll make."

"Commotion!" the Marquis exclaimed.

"Well, the staff'll think it odd you ridin' off. It'd be a great mistake if it was talked about in the drawing rooms and, if it appeared in the newspapers, then you'd no longer be disguised."

"You are quite right, Herbert, I had not thought of that. In fact it is very clever of you. I will leave from the Mews quite early so that they will merely think I am going into Hyde Park."

He thought for a moment and then added,

"If you go there earlier still, you can saddle Samson and put the saddle bags with my clothes on either side of him without the grooms being aware of it."

"That's just what I be thinkin' of myself, my Lord. The quicker you ride out of London, the better."

The Marquis did not answer.

He was ruminating that the ride to Northumberland would undoubtedly be a bore and that he had been rather a fool in taking up the challenge offered to him by the Duke of Dunstead.

However, it was much too late now to go back on his word and he could only hope that he would be able to reach Northumberland in record time and then be able to return, if necessary, by sea.

"It should not be too difficult for you to find a ship which will take you up to Shermont Castle, Herbert. There are always ships en route for Edinburgh, although I don't expect you will find them very comfortable."

"Your Lordship needn't worry about me," Herbert answered. "All you have to worry about is yourself, my Lord, and I only wish I was comin' with you."

The Marquis laughed.

"I think they would be rather surprised if I did the bet disguised as Mr. Barlow who could not go anywhere without his valet!"

Herbert, however, was not amused.

"I'm talkin' seriously, my Lord. So you must take care of yourself. I don't like to think of you alone on the roads at night, so stop at some safe inn afore it gets dark."

"I will certainly do so," the Marquis promised. "In fact in the dark I am likely to lose my way. I have, as you well know, been North a number of times, but only as far as Doncaster to see my horses run."

"And very successful they turned out to be the last time, my Lord."

The Marquis smiled.

"I was very proud of them and very pleased with myself for owning them. It will seem very strange to only own one horse, which must not be a spectacular one."

He had specially chosen Samson, who actually had won several Classic races, simply because he did not look so stylish as some of the other horses he owned.

The stallions he rode in the Park were outstanding, but Samson, although he was very fast, did not attract the same attention as those that were far slower than he was.

The Marquis greatly enjoyed his bath in front of the fireplace.

Then, putting on his best evening clothes, he turned to Herbert,

"I have forgotten for the moment which invitation to dinner I accepted for tonight."

"As it so happens, my Lord, you refused the dinner parties and are dinin' alone with her Ladyship."

"Oh, yes, so I am. It slipped my mind. Actually I thought it was the Devonshires I was expected at."

"No, that's tomorrow night, my Lord, and I'll have to make a good excuse for your Lordship not bein' there."

"Yes, of course it is, how stupid of me, but so much seems to be happening at once and unless you remind me, Herbert, I will make a thousand mistakes."

"I can't remind you if I'm not with your Lordship," Herbert parried. "But you did promise Lady Cowleigh that you would dine with her alone."

The Marquis remembered now and he recalled as well that Lord Cowleigh had an important engagement in the country.

Lady Cowleigh was someone new he had pursued with some difficulty for the past two weeks.

She had managed to be elusive, which made it all the more interesting.

He had been surprised when she had told him the day before yesterday that she would be very delighted if he would dine with her, as her husband was away on business.

He had in fact been so surprised that she had at last succumbed to his invitations that it was unusual and indeed very remiss of him to have forgotten her.

'It would happen,' he thought, 'just as I am leaving London and I am sure that I will find her irresistible.'

He then found himself wondering if it would be a mistake to start another *affaire-de-coeur.*

He would then be obliged tomorrow to send her a message to say that he had been called away and so he was not certain when they would be able to meet again.

He was far too experienced not to realise that this would annoy her considerably and it was very doubtful if she would be waiting for him on his return.

On the other hand, it was impossible to say at the last moment that he was unable to keep the appointment he had made and she would be quite right if she then felt that he had let her down in a most unfeeling manner.

He was silent as Herbert helped him into his very smartly cut waistcoat and his cut-away evening coat made him look even more dashing than he had in the daytime.

"How can I be such a fool," the Marquis said aloud, "as to have forgotten where I was going tonight?"

"It's understandable when your Lordship has had so many invitations," Herbert said soothingly. "You'll enjoy yourself, my Lord, with her Ladyship. I've seen pictures of her in the magazines and she's very beautiful. There be no other word to describe her."

"You are right, Herbert, and so I would be a fool to miss the opportunity of being alone with her."

The Marquis looked in the mirror to see if his hair was tidy and the top of his handkerchief showed from the pocket of his coat.

Then he said,

"Don't forget to send the usual bouquet of orchids to her Ladyship tomorrow morning. I will find time before I leave to write and tell her I have been called away owing to the illness of one of my closest relatives, who may not have long to live."

"That's the right story, my Lord. There be no one born who couldn't be real sympathetic if you was in that position."

The Marquis could have told him that there were a number of women who were very suspicious when he had used this excuse and had told him so in no uncertain terms.

However, he only hoped that Lady Cowleigh would be different.

Then he turned towards the door and said,

"Call me early, however sleepy I may be, and don't forget I want the plainest clothes to travel in so that I look rather dull and insignificant."

"I'll do me best, my Lord. At the same time, if you asks me, it'll be difficult to make you look anythin' but the smart handsome gentleman you've always been!"

The Marquis smiled but did not reply.

In fact before Herbert had finished speaking, he had reached the top of the stairs.

His closed carriage was waiting for him at the front of the house driven by two horses.

He was wondering if he should keep it or walk back home as he often did. It was a fine night and he knew that, if the evening developed as he expected, he would enjoy the fresh air and the last twinkle from the stars in the sky.

Then, as he drove off, he thought that it might be too tiring to walk from Lady Cowleigh's house to his own.

It would shorten the sleep he would definitely need before he set out on his arduous journey in the morning.

Therefore, when he arrived at Cowleigh House, he instructed the coachman to come back in two hours' time.

He was amused at the expression on the man's face.

He had been certain that to disguise what time he left the lady in question, he would have been prepared to walk back to Belgrave Square.

Then, as he was let into the house by a superior-looking elderly butler, he doubted for the first time, if on such a short acquaintance Lady Cowleigh would succumb to his advances.

Because of his successes in the past, he had never been sent away when he wished to stay.

But now, for the first time, he was wondering if he was over-optimistic in thinking that she would not play the old game of being surprised at his suggestions.

She would make him, as she might well think, even more ardent and keen than he was already by prolonging the moment when she accepted his advances.

As he went up the stairs to the drawing room, he found himself wondering how the evening would end.

Would it be any different from what he anticipated?

The butler announced him in a stentorian voice,

"The Marquis of Whisinford, my Lady."

As the Marquis suspected, she was wearing not a full evening dress but a most attractive negligee. It was of a pale green chiffon ornamented with gold lace and round her neck was a glittering necklace of diamonds and in her ears there were some superlative emeralds.

She did not rise from the sofa she was reclining on when he was announced, but held out her hand.

Raising it to his lips he gently kissed each finger one by one.

"You look even more beautiful than you did the other night," he greeted her.

"I am so glad you could come tonight, my Lord, so that we can talk without being interrupted,"

"And what in particular have we to talk about?" the Marquis enquired.

As he was speaking, he helped himself to a glass of champagne from a bottle in an impressive ice-bucket.

She did not reply and he raised his glass.

"Let me drink," he said, "to the loveliest woman I have ever seen, who I wish to see a great deal more of."

It was what he had said many times and which had always been received gracefully.

"Lady Cowleigh's eyes fluttered most becomingly and she smiled before she breathed seductively,

"I am sure you always flatter everyone, my Lord, and that is why you are so popular."

"Am I popular?" the Marquis enquired. "I am often told I have a great number of enemies, but I must admit that they are usually the husbands of very beautiful women who, until I appear, did not appreciate their beauty!"

Lady Cowleigh laughed.

"I cannot say that of my husband and I can tell you that he is very jealous and very quick at reaching for his duelling pistol."

"Now you are trying to frighten me," the Marquis said. "But I think your husband is very wise in guarding you as I would do if you were my wife."

There was a slight pause and then Lady Cowleigh reflected,

"I wonder if anyone would really be happy as your wife. I expect that you are well aware, my Lord, that your reputation is a very questionable one to say the least of it."

"You must not believe all the gossip you hear. In fact, at least eighty per cent of it is totally exaggerated or completely untrue."

Lady Cowleigh laughed again.

"That is a very clever way of disregarding the fact that you are openly talked about as being a roué, which is unusual in someone so young."

"As I have just said, you must not believe all you hear. Equally you must believe me when I tell you that you are very beautiful."

It was true because she had a very unusual beauty.

In most of his love affairs the Marquis had been attracted by women with golden hair and blue eyes and he also greatly admired the perfect pink and white complexion for which English women were noted.

Lady Cowleigh on the other hand had dark hair and eyes which, when he looked closely at them, were a deep green.

That she was proud of them was shown by the way she sported her emeralds and was wearing a green dress that made her skin seem even whiter than it was naturally.

It accentuated the darkness of her hair and she was certainly, he reflected, different from any other woman he had been attracted to.

The sublime whiteness of her skin reminded him of the snow-tipped mountains he had seen when he visited Switzerland.

When dinner was announced, he found it was being served in a small room opposite the drawing room in which there were a great number of flower arrangements.

They were put there, he realised, to hide what was otherwise quite obviously a study and he suspected that it was where his Lordship, when he was in residence, wrote his letters and read the newspapers.

"I thought it was a mistake," Lady Cowleigh said, "to have to go upstairs to the big dining room as it always seems to me cold and too large when I am alone or have only one guest."

"I think that this room is delightful and a perfect background for you," the Marquis said automatically.

It was something he had said a hundred times and the words came to his lips without him even thinking.

He was aware as the food, which was delicious, was served by the butler who let him in, that the rest of the household were not expected to know about his presence.

They might talk and talk in Mayfair flowed very quickly from one house to another and from one beauty to another.

The Marquis knew that if one of his former beauties with whom he had had an *affaire-de-coeur* was aware that he was now with Lady Cowleigh, they would undoubtedly spread the message all over London Society.

It would then only be a question of time before his Lordship, one way or another, would hear it.

He therefore thoroughly enjoyed dinner and found that Lady Cowleigh was amusing and able to keep him laughing until the meal ended.

Then, as they walked back into the drawing room, he was aware, as he closed the door, that behind him the lights were dimmer than they had been when he arrived.

There was a door at the far end of the room, which he was almost certain would lead into her bedroom.

Just for a short moment he hesitated, remembering the long road North that lay in front of him tomorrow.

Then he thought that a bird in the hand was worth two in the bush and perhaps never again would there be an opportunity like this.

It was as he closed the door into the dining room behind him and then saw that Lady Cowleigh was standing waiting for him by the fireplace, that he knew exactly what his next move would be.

As he took her gently into his arms, he realised that everything was moving exactly as he expected, step by step towards her bedroom.

*

It was around three hours later that the Marquis remembered that his carriage would be waiting for him.

"You are not leaving me?" Lady Cowleigh asked. "Oh, dearest, there is no hurry and you have made me so very very happy."

"Just as you have made me," the Marquis breathed. "But unfortunately I have to leave London early tomorrow morning."

"Leave London!" Lady Cowleigh cried. "But you know I want to see you and Arthur will not be home until the end of the week."

"I learnt today," he replied, "that unfortunately one of my relatives is very ill, in fact dying. As she wishes to say a final goodbye to me before she leaves this world, I really cannot refuse. So I must go to her tomorrow."

"Oh, why must all this happen just when we are so happy?" Lady Cowleigh asked.

"That is the same question I am asking myself," the Marquis assured her. "But I will be as quick as possible and I will let you know the moment I can return."

She gave a little sob and turned her face against his shoulder.

It was another ten minutes before he could manage to escape from her hands and her lips and started to dress.

"I never thought that this would happen to me," she said. "I cannot bear you to leave me."

"I have no wish to leave you," the Marquis replied. "But I will not be away for long, then I will get in touch with you immediately."

"I will be very upset," she murmured, "in fact in tears if you do not do so."

He finished dressing himself and from long practice he was very skilful at it.

Then he turned towards the large canopied four-poster the bed.

She looked very lovely in the light of three candles that were all that illuminated the room.

He had been aware that the large amount of lilies and the scent of them could not have been arranged for any woman occupying the huge bed alone.

It passed through his mind that he was certainly not the first, nor the last, who would be entertained so cleverly and so comfortably.

The Marquis walked towards the bed and she held out her hands.

He took one of them and kissed her fingers as he had done when he arrived.

Then he said,

"Sleep well, my beautiful one, and then if you must dream – dream of me."

"I have no wish to dream when you are near me," Lady Cowleigh sighed. "It is still too early for you to go, so send your carriage away and stay with me."

"I wish I could do that, but as I have just told you, I have to leave early in the morning. It would be a disaster if I was too sleepy to do so."

He kissed her again.

When she rose in the bed as if to hold him in both arms, he moved swiftly towards the door.

"I cannot let you leave!" she cried.

But it was too late.

He was gone before she had finished speaking.

As she now heard him running down the stairs, she threw herself back petulantly against the pillows.

She was furious that he had got away so easily, but at the same time she was certain he would come back.

There had never been a lover who had not found her irresistible and she was quite certain that the Marquis would be no exception.

Driving back to his house in Belgrave Square, the Marquis thought that it was a good thing he was leaving London tomorrow – or was it today?

He could not explain to himself why, but he knew without putting it into words that he really had no wish to see her again.

It did surprise him, as it would undoubtedly horrify and astonish her, but he could not understand why.

He was not enraptured with her as he should be.

In fact there was, the Marquis thought, nothing new or unusual about their lovemaking except that almost for the first time in an *affaire-de-coeur* he was content to leave it and not pursue the matter any further.

It was indeed something that had not happened to him before and he found it hard to express, even to himself, what he felt.

Yet he knew instinctively that he had no desire to see Lady Cowleigh again, beautiful though she was.

Perhaps it was because everything was too carefully planned – too perfect in its own way and therefore there was nothing unusual or irresistible in their lovemaking.

She was beautiful, as beautiful in her own way as any woman he had known before.

But he had to be honest and admit that there was something lacking, something that made him glad that he was now going home.

It was still not too late in the evening for him to have a good sleep before he left tomorrow morning.

'Why? Why do I feel like this?' he asked himself.

But there was no answer to the question.

As he arrived in Belgrave Square, he was glad to be back and it seemed as though the house protected him.

Herbert was not waiting up for him because he had strict instructions not to do so and it was arranged that only if the Marquis rang for him was he to get out of bed and go to assist him to undress.

It was something that had never happened before and the Marquis had no wish for it to happen now.

At the same time, as he climbed into his own bed, he asked himself, as he had asked himself over and over again when driving home, why he had no wish to stay with the beautiful Lady Cowleigh?

Or why he had no desire to see her again?

'I must be getting old and blasé,' he thought before he climbed into bed.

*

He slept peacefully and he was not in the least tired when he heard Herbert come into his room.

"What time is it?" he asked.

"Six o'clock, my Lord," Herbert replied, "and you must remember you're havin' breakfast with His Grace at seven o'clock."

"Oh, yes, so I am," the Marquis exclaimed, "and it would be a great mistake for me to be late!"

"That's what I thought, my Lord, and I've been to the stables and Samson be ready for you."

The Marquis knew that this meant Herbert had not arranged for one of the grooms to bring his horse round to the front door.

When he had washed, he found that Herbert had put out clothes that he did not remember owning.

He had not altered in size or height for the last few years and he guessed that they were clothes he had worn when exploring with two of his friends in Nepal.

They certainly looked worn.

Yet, as they had been made by a good, if not over-expensive tailor, they were certainly just what Neil Barlow, whoever he might be, would wear.

When he had dressed, he looked at himself in the mirror.

He thought that he certainly looked very middle-class, owning one horse and having very little money.

Then he laughed because it was a way he had never thought of himself as appearing.

He enjoyed the compliments he always received in being one of the smartest young men in Mayfair.

"I thinks you'll find everything you could want, my Lord," Herbert said. "You'll find a small pistol in the right hand bag with your shoes."

"I had not thought of my shoes," the Marquis said. "But I will certainly need them as these old boots look as though I have worn them a thousand times already."

"That's what your Lordship had when I bought you some new ones. You've rode a great many miles in those boots and they show it as if it was written on them."

This was true enough and the Marquis laughed.

"I am most grateful to you, Herbert. Equally I will be very glad when I see you again with something decent to wear. I don't suppose that Mr. Neil Barlow ever had a valet like you, as you are unique!"

Herbert smiled at the compliment he had received many times before.

"I know one thing, my Lord, Mr. Neil Barlow will need my services by the time he reaches Shermont Castle."

"Well, mind you are there when I arrive. I cannot believe that my cousin would let me to borrow his clothes, being an unexpected and perhaps unwelcome visitor."

"You'd never be that, my Lord," Herbert protested. "If you asks me, they'll be waiting with open arms for you at Shermont Castle."

"I hope you are right, Herbert. If I am late, don't worry, I will turn up sooner or later."

"Now don't you go on frightenin' me. You knows, my Lord, how much you mean to me and to all of us who serves you. If you was in trouble, there'd not be a dry eye in the kitchen."

"That is the nicest compliment I have ever had," the Marquis said. "Now come on. I must arrive at the Duke's on time otherwise he might think I am backing out."

"I thinks it'd be a good thing if you did, but I'll be crossin' my fingers and hopin' everythin' will be all right till your Lordship gets home."

"You must not worry about me, Herbert. I will turn up like a bad penny and expect everything to be in order as it always is."

He ran down the stairs and Herbert followed him more slowly.

As the Marquis was expected to do, he slipped out of the back door and across the small garden which led to the Mews.

There was no one about at this early hour and when he reached the Mews, he found that there was only one sleepy groom in charge of Samson.

The Marquis wasted no time in mounting his horse.

As he did so, he saw Herbert coming through the garden door.

He saluted him with his whip and Herbert waved his arm. They did not speak and the Marquis rode off into the street at the bottom of the Mews.

It did not take long to reach the Duke of Dunstead's house in Berkeley Square.

When he reached it, he saw tethered outside a horse that was almost as good as Samson and he knew that it was one that his friend Alfred especially prized.

'He must,' the Marquis thought, 'be anxious to win this bet. Otherwise he would not take that particular horse on such a lengthy journey.'

A groom appeared to take his horse from him and he walked into the house.

The Duke was waiting for him in the dining room where Lord Alfred was already eating a hearty breakfast.

"I thought that you must have forgotten us," Alfred said as the Marquis walked in.

"Is it likely that I should?" the Marquis asked. "I have my eye on one of His Grace's horses which I am very anxious to own."

The Duke chuckled.

"Optimism will get you a long way," he said. "But remember that your adventure has to be real and not part of your imagination."

"If you are suggesting, Your Grace, that we could become liars," the Marquis cajoled, "then you are much mistaken. We would never lie over anything as important as a bet made in White's."

They all laughed at this and then the Duke said,

"I should hope not, but I am sceptical and before I part with any of my best horses I will want proof of what adventure you have encountered and perhaps someone to assure me that it was, in fact, a *real* adventure."

"But you may have to take our word for it," the Marquis said lightly. "But I can tell you I will be strictly truthful. If I lose, I lose! All the same I intend to win!"

"So do I," Alfred chimed in.

"What really pleases me," the Duke remarked, "is that you both seem very enthusiastic. I rather expected that you might back out at the last moment."

"How could we ever do such a thing," the Marquis asked with mock severity, "if the bet was made at White's, although secret at this moment, it will later appear in the famous Betting Book."

"I had not thought of that," the Duke said. "But undoubtedly it should have a place there if, in fact, you are successful."

"I have every intention of being so!" Alfred said. "Although I cannot imagine how I will find an adventure on the road to Land's End, but then one never knows ones luck."

"That is exactly what you two are trying to find," the Duke affirmed.

They laughed and talked on during breakfast which was certainly an impressive meal to start the day with.

As they were joking away, the Marquis saw the Duke look speculatively at the clock and realised that they should be off.

"Come along, Alfred," he suggested. "Let's start our adventure and the quicker it is over the quicker we can come back to civilisation."

"Of course," Alfred agreed, "with our heads held high and the banners unfurled to show that we have won a victory."

"That is just what I hope you will do," the Duke said. "But do remember I don't want you to take any risks. That is why, looking as you do, I don't think that you will be captured by footpads or, indeed, be pursued by beautiful women!"

The Marquis and Alfred both laughed.

"One thing is quite certain," the Marquis said, "no one would take us for millionaires and I would not be at all surprised if we came back to tell you that we have not only failed to find adventure but we have been ignored by every woman who looked in our direction!"

"Which will be very good for both of you if it really happens," the Duke observed.

Equally he thought to himself that the Marquis was so handsome that women would be looking at his face and not at his clothes.

They were still laughing amongst themselves when the Duke urged,

"Come along, it's time you were off! Good luck to you both. I will pray that you will come home safely with an exciting story to tell me."

"The trouble is that you are more optimistic than we are," the Marquis answered. "I believe that you should be taking part in this game and I am quite certain that you would have a real tale to tell while we will be hard-pushed to impress you."

"If I was thirty years younger, I would undoubtedly accept your challenge," the Duke replied. "As it is, I will stay at home and speculate as to what is happening to you."

When they reached their horses, he then shook their hands warmly and said,

"Good luck and God bless you! As I am certain that you will be successful, I will keep my best horses out of sight!"

"If we are not allowed to cheat, you are not allowed to either," the Marquis cautioned. "I promise you that my story, if there is one, will be true from start to finish."

"And I promise the same," Alfred agreed. "But I bet that Neil's story will involve a very pretty girl. They will drop down from Heaven for him, while I will be left to search the bushes for mine!"

"Now you are trying to seek false sympathy and understanding," the Marquis teased him. "That is strictly forbidden in the rules, is it not, Your Grace?"

"Quite right," the Duke said. "I will be waiting anxiously for your return."

By this time they were both mounted and, as they rode away, the Duke waved to them and they waved back.

"He really is a sporting old boy," the Marquis said when they were out of earshot. "I believe we are giving him a great deal of pleasure if nothing else."

"I thought just the same," Alfred replied. "We will have to make up some sort of story to please him if no one else."

"Oh, I am sure something will turn up. As far as I am concerned, the quicker I can get to Northumberland the better."

"I feel the same about Land's End," Lord Alfred answered. "I was remembering last night that it is well known as a refuge for smugglers. So perhaps you will find that I have been smuggled to some European country!"

The Marquis laughed.

"I think they are far more interested in goods that can be sold than in young men who usually want money without any attachment to it."

"That is exactly what I want," Alfred agreed.

"Then goodbye and good luck!" the Marquis said. "This is where we part company and I take the road to the North."

Just for a moment Alfred looked rather gloomy at the South road ahead of him.

"I wish we were going together," he said. "That would be fun and we would be able to joke."

"Why did you not think of it before?"

"Because I knew that the Duke had thought it all out in his own mind. He expects that we should be more likely to have some dramatic encounter if we were alone than if we were together."

"I suppose you are right, but I agree with you that it would be fun to go together. If this expedition fails, I will take you on a trip to the top of Mont Blanc or we could be less arduous and enjoy ourselves with the 'soiled doves'."

"I am not overwhelmed at either invitation," Alfred replied.

He turned his horse and called out,

"Goodbye, old boy, and don't get into mischief!"

"Goodbye," the Marquis replied. "See you in two or three weeks' time."

He thought as he spoke and pointed Samson in the other direction that he was being optimistic.

There was no chance of them completing this rather ridiculous bet in under three weeks to say the least of it.

It might easily take over a month.

Then, as he could see that the winding road ahead was empty and it was not yet as hot as it would be later in the day, he started Samson off at a good gallop.

The stallion was only too eager to show his paces.

They travelled for over a mile without the Marquis drawing him in.

Then, as they slowed down and the sunshine made everything seem so inviting, the Marquis began to hum to himself a tune he had enjoyed at *Drury Lane Theatre* a week ago.

CHAPTER THREE

The Marquis was feeling hungry when he reached a small village.

At the top of the village green he saw a rather nice-looking old inn.

He rode up to it and then found when he entered the yard at the back that there was a stable available for horses.

He put Samson inside and saw that he had plenty to eat and fresh water.

Then he walked into the inn and, as he expected, it was quite small and obviously built a century or so before.

There was an elderly publican in the bar and the Marquis asked if he could order some food for luncheon.

The publican was delighted at having a customer and he enquired whether he would rather sit outside or in.

The Marquis decided that inside was likely to be quicker and more comfortable and the publican showed into a small room where there were three tables, each one able to seat three or four people.

He asked the publican to bring him whatever they had available and this turned out to be a good dish of meat, potatoes and an array of green vegetables.

When he had finished, there was then cheese and he found one which he thought must be local and which was as good as anything he had eaten in London.

The Marquis had made a golden rule a long time ago never to drink when he was riding and so he asked for cider that the publican told him proudly was made nearby.

When he had finished his luncheon, he asked the publican if he was busy.

"We does fairly well on a Saturday night," he said, "but as you can see it's quiet durin' the week. The old 'uns come in later on in the evenin' to 'ave a glass of beer, but otherwise, sir, there ain't much excitement in this part of the world."

The Marquis paid for his luncheon and tipped the publican generously who was astonished.

Then he collected Samson, who was now obviously well rested and so he set off at a good pace and must have gone for nearly two miles and seen little traffic on the road.

Then on a straight stretch, where he could see for nearly half a mile, he became aware that there was a horse behind him.

The Marquis was not riding at a particularly fast pace at that stage and a moment or so later the horse drew level with him.

He turned his head to see a young girl riding what he recognised at once was a well bred horse.

She was close beside him and he looked at her in some surprise, thinking that there was plenty of room on the empty road for both of them.

Then she spoke in a hesitating and shy voice,

"Would you mind – very much, sir, if I rode beside – you?"

The Marquis looked at her again.

"Is there any reason why you should ask that?" he enquired.

She looked over her shoulder in an anxious way.

"It seems as if you are running away," the Marquis then remarked.

"That is exactly – what I am doing," she replied, "and it will help me considerably – if I can ride with you up this long straight road."

The Marquis was curious and then he said,

"I do not wish to seem impertinent, but I would like to know why."

"I will tell you if we can – go a little faster," the girl answered him nervously.

The Marquis's horse was only too willing and so was hers. They rode on for half a mile without speaking.

Then, as the road ahead twisted and turned a little, the Marquis pulled in Samson and suggested,

"Now I think you are safe from prying eyes, if that is what you are afraid of. You did promise to tell me why you wished to accompany me, for which, of course, I am very honoured."

He spoke somewhat sarcastically thinking it odd for a young woman, who was quite obviously a lady, to be out on the road alone.

And certainly to be talking to a strange man she did not know.

He realised as he looked at her again that she was, in point of fact, extremely pretty.

She turned her head and looked back anxiously.

"I feel I am safer – now," she sighed. "But, if I had been riding alone, it would have been obvious to anyone looking for me – that it was me."

She put it in an almost childlike way and then the Marquis laughed.

"Why are you running away?" he quizzed her.

"I am running away – as quickly as I possibly can," the girl replied. "I am afraid that my stepfather will have sent his men – to bring me back."

"Your stepfather?" the Marquis echoed. "What is he doing to frighten you so much that you ran away?"

The girl drew in her breath.

"He is determined I will marry – one of his friends who is a horrible beastly man and I have no wish to marry him – or anyone else for that matter."

The Marquis rode on a little while before he asked,

"So you are running away from your home. Is that wise?"

"I am going to one of my aunts, who has always been very kind to me and is, in fact, also my Godmother. She lives in Yorkshire."

The Marquis stared at her.

"You are riding to Yorkshire alone!"

"It is the only way I can get there and I did not dare take a servant with me for fear she would tell my stepfather that I was leaving."

"But you do realise that Yorkshire is a very long way away? And it is most certainly not safe for any young woman, especially one riding a well bred horse, to be alone on such a long journey."

"I know that, sir. Of course I know that," the girl replied. "But what else – am I to do? If I had stayed at home, I would have been engaged – to this dreadful man, whether I liked it or not. Then there might have been – no way of escape."

She spoke with a distinct note in her voice that told the Marquis she was really frightened and she obviously loathed the man her stepfather had chosen for her.

They rode for a little while in silence, although not as fast as previously, because the road twisted.

Then the Marquis observed,

"I would suspect, as you are under age, that your stepfather is your Guardian."

"Yes, and I must obey him until I am twenty-one," the girl answered. "He has told me that often enough. He made it quite clear this morning that the man I loathe and detest was coming to stay and I had to accept his offer of marriage, whether I liked it or not."

"Under these circumstances," the Marquis said, "I think you have been very wise and brave to run away."

"Do you really think so?" she exclaimed. "You are so kind and sensible. Everyone else keeps telling me what I should do and it's always – just what I don't want to do myself."

The Marquis smiled.

"I am afraid that happens to all of us."

"I will not marry the man my stepfather has chosen for me! I hate him and I would much rather die than be his wife."

She spoke with a violence that made the Marquis look at her.

She had a small build and was very light on her horse. And she was exceedingly pretty.

He could easily understand any man being eager to make her his wife.

Aloud he asked,

"Are you quite certain that your aunt in Yorkshire, who you are going to, will protect you?"

"She has never got on well with my stepfather and will, I am quite certain, when I tell her what is happening, be shocked at him behaving in such a hard and cruel way. She has asked me to stay several times, but he would not let me go to her because they did not get on together."

She paused before she added positively,

"I know that she will fight him for my sake and ask the rest of the family to support me."

"Then we must make certain that you travel safely to Yorkshire," the Marquis replied.

"You are very kind to let me ride with you," the girl said. "I can only hope that if, as I think very probable, my stepfather has sent his men to search for me, they will be looking for a woman alone."

"I think it is very clever of you to think of that," the Marquis remarked. "As I too am alone, I am delighted to have your company."

She smiled at him.

"I knew from the horse you were riding that you were the sort of gentleman I could ask such a favour from."

The Marquis laughed.

"It is indeed the first time that Samson has been a representative of my behaviour. Of course, I am sure he is very flattered!"

The girl laughed too and then she asked,

"Please help me if you can to get to Yorkshire very quickly. I have travelled on this road before, but I did not notice the way particularly and I am frightened of taking the wrong turning."

"I will not let you do that. I am going to Yorkshire and then on to Northumberland. Now I suggest, as you are running away, that we ride as fast as we can for five or so miles. Then, if you are being followed, they will probably think you have turned off and are not heading North."

"I hope they will think that," the girl said. "At the same time I have a feeling that Step-Papa will guess where I have gone and will therefore be following me."

"Then the quicker we move the better," the Marquis answered.

He gave Samson his head and they set off at a good pace and the girl was having little difficulty in keeping up with him.

They must have ridden for about four miles before the Marquis slowed down and cautioned,

"I think that we should be very careful where we stay tonight."

The girl drew in her breath.

"I thought of that and I know it would seem very strange for me to go to a hotel or inn alone. I was thinking perhaps I would have to sleep in a ditch or in a wood."

"I think that would be extremely uncomfortable," the Marquis remarked. "What I was thinking was that they would not expect you to stay at a small and remote inn. Therefore, as it is getting on in the afternoon, we should look for a little village which your followers would think was not smart enough for you."

He was wondering, as he was speaking, if he should ask her name and who her parents had been.

Then he thought she would expect to want to know his and he somehow disliked lying to anyone who was as young and pretty as the girl riding beside him.

"You are so sensible," she said, "and I am so lucky to have found you. I feel sure if I had been alone I would have done the wrong thing and gone to a hotel in a small town."

She gave a little laugh before she added,

"I was really thinking of my stallion, Fireball, who is very particular where he lays his head."

The Marquis laughed.

"I am sure that Samson feels the same!"

"Oh, that is an excellent name for him! He is just magnificent," the girl said. "I am sure Fireball is charmed to meet him."

"Well, as they are introduced to each other," the Marquis replied, "perhaps we should do the same. As you are in disguise, you need only tell me your Christian name and I will tell you that mine is Neil."

"And mine is Velina and I am so glad to meet you."

"Now we are formally introduced to each other," the Marquis announced, "the sooner that we ride on and find somewhere to rest our heads the better."

"On behalf of Fireball I am very grateful to you," Velina said solemnly. "I was worrying about how I could possibly give him good food if I had to sleep in a ditch."

"I cannot imagine anything more uncomfortable for both of you. I am sure that we will find a nice inn where we can be well looked after and safe."

"I am praying that is true," Velina said, "and now because we are still near home I am worried about the men following me and I would like to go a little faster."

The Marquis did not bother to answer her.

He merely allowed Samson to gallop as fast as he could and Fireball had no trouble keeping up with him.

It was now nearly seven o'clock and the Marquis was wondering what had happened to local small villages when they came to one which he thought looked ideal.

There was a Norman Church, a few houses and a number of picturesque thatched cottages.

He looked for an inn and found it on the other side of the village.

It was on the traditional green and there were several old men sitting outside smoking and drinking beer.

They rode round to the back of the inn.

As the Marquis expected, there was the usual yard and quite a large stable which, with satisfaction, he realised was empty.

They put their horses into separate horseboxes and then while he was unsaddling Samson, Velina was doing the same to Fireball.

In fact she was so expert at it that the Marquis knew that she must, when she was at home, look after her own horse instead of leaving it to a servant.

He brought in fresh water from the pump in the yard and saw that there was plenty of food in the mangers.

Carrying one of the bags that Herbert had attached to the saddle, he looked to see if Velina was ready.

She was also carrying a saddlebag, but it was very much larger and fuller than his.

She saw him glance at it and said,

"I brought as little as possible with me, but I will not have to eat dinner in my riding clothes, which I am finding are rather heavy."

"I think it will be difficult to have a bath if you are thinking of that," the Marquis commented.

They were walking out of the stable yard when he stopped.

"I have just thought, he said, "that it will be very difficult for you to stay here with a different name to mine. It will also, apart from anything else, make the publican curious."

"I did not think of that!" Velina exclaimed. "What shall we do?"

"I suggest that I say you are my sister," the Marquis answered.

He almost added that, if he said they were married, they would be expected to share a room. He felt it would be not only an unnecessary remark but would make Velina feel shy.

"Oh, you are clever!" she replied. "And I am very delighted to be your sister. I often wanted one myself."

"I might say the same," the Marquis added. "I was the only child and would have loved to have had brothers and sisters to play with."

They had reached the door into the inn and, pushing it open, they found themselves in a passage that led past the kitchen to the front of the building.

An elderly man came out of what was obviously the bar and offered,

"Can I do anything for you, sir?"

"My sister and I would be grateful if we could stay with you for the night," the Marquis replied. "We are on our way to the North and it will soon be too dark to go any further."

The publican scratched his head.

"Well, we've got two rooms," he said, "but we're not often asked for 'em and so you might not think 'em very comfortable."

The Marquis was rather surprised that he should be expected to want comfortable rooms.

He had no idea that because he looked so handsome and dignified, his well-worn clothes were not really a very good disguise.

"I am sure they will give us a good night's sleep," he said.

"I 'opes so," the publican replied.

He went a few steps down the passage and shouted,

"Missus! 'Ere be two guests who wants to stay the night with us. Come and look after 'em."

"I'm comin', I'm comin'," a woman replied.

She came out of the kitchen, wiping her hands on her apron and said to the Marquis,

"We don't often 'ave visitors who stays the night because there be an 'otel just down the road."

The Marquis had noted it when they passed it some minutes ago and he thought then that it was just the type of hotel the usual traveller would stay in.

"I think your inn looks delightful," he said aloud. "I am sure that you will be able to give my sister and me something nice for dinner."

"We'll do our best, sir," the woman answered going ahead of them. "But, as me 'usband said we don't 'ave many visitors who wants to stay 'ere. They just drinks and be orf."

The Marquis smiled at this and then he realised that Velina was smiling too.

At the same time he thought that the inn was just what they wanted, somewhere where no one would expect to find them. And at least they would be able to have a peaceful night.

The rooms were small but clean and the beds were not entirely comfortable, but at least, he reckoned, Velina would feel safe.

"There be water in yon jug," the publican's wife was saying, "but if you wants it 'ot you'll 'ave to come and fetch it from the kitchen."

"I expect we can manage with cold for now," the Marquis replied, "and then ask you for some hot when we go to bed."

"That you shall 'ave," the woman promised. "Now I must 'urry back to make you somethin' warmin' for your evenin' meal."

She was gone before he could reply.

The Marquis smiled at Velina before he took the room where the window overlooked the stable yard and he left her to have the one with the view of the green.

"We are lucky," she said as she went into the room. "If there was anyone else staying here, we would have had to go on further."

"I think that I am the lucky one in finding *you*," the Marquis replied with a smile.

It was the sort of answer he would have made to any woman because it was polite and pleasant.

But Velina gave a little cry.

"You must not say that yet! If we are lucky to be sure of anything, it is that you have been kind and helpful to me. But we have still have a long way to go."

"I know that," the Marquis affirmed. "But forget about that at the moment and think about your dinner."

He went into his own room as he spoke, but then he heard her laughing.

'I wonder,' he said to himself, 'if the Duke would count this as an adventure? It is certainly something I did not expect.'

He washed and brushed his hair.

Looking at himself in the small mirror on the chest of drawers, he decided that no one would suspect him of being anyone but just an ordinary countryman or perhaps a salesman of cheap goods.

But then he had no idea that Velina was already thinking of him as a gentleman.

'He must have perhaps lost his money and is going North to find a job,' she thought, 'which is not available to him in the South.'

It was strange that he had such a magnificent horse, but he might have had it loaned to him or he had perhaps sold everything he possessed to buy Samson.

'Anyway,' she told herself, 'he is very kind and I would never have managed if I had not met him.'

She felt herself shiver at the thought that she would have been too frightened to go to an inn all on her own, as she had always understood that a woman travelling alone would not be allowed to stay at a respectable hostelry.

She took off her hat and her jacket and then decided that she would be much more comfortable if she took off her boots and put on one of the dresses she had packed in her saddlebag.

She was quite certain that her aunt would buy her new clothes when she eventually reached Yorkshire and it would be too hot to sit down to dinner in her riding clothes.

The Marquis, waiting for her in the small dining room, was wondered why she took so long.

He had not expected her to change and, when she walked in, he was astounded at how pretty she was.

In fact, it was right to say beautiful.

Her hair, which was naturally curly, was very fair and she had brushed it into place and arranged it neatly at the back of her head. Nevertheless small curls fell neatly into place near her forehead on the side of her cheeks.

It had been difficult to look at her when they were riding so fast.

He saw now that her eyes were not the pale blue of the forget-me-nots, but the deep blue of the Mediterranean and her skin was exactly as it should be, pink and white.

There was no doubt that she was not only beautiful but exceedingly well born.

Her dress was plain and of very thin material which made it easy to pack and had not creased in the saddlebag. It was very pale green and the white collar might have been the colour of snowdrops.

"I am sorry if I kept you waiting," Velina said as she sat down opposite him.

"I have had already two glasses of a rather good sherry," he replied. "What would you like, Velina?"

"I expect there will be some cider, although I would rather have lemonade if they have it."

The Marquis left the dining room to go to the bar, where there were young men asking for glasses of beer.

The publican hurried to fetch the lemonade Velina had asked for and the Marquis decided that he would drink it too.

He felt sure that any wine offered by the inn would be cheap and unpleasant and, as he had an excellent cellar of his own, he disliked cheap wine of any sort.

Dinner was rather what he expected.

There was a rabbit soup, which was quite pleasant and this was followed by roast chicken, but with nothing to go with it and it proved to be rather dull.

He was, however, much more interested in Velina than in anything else and they talked about pictures, books and, of course, horses.

He found that Velina was very interested in racing and she had not had any chance, she told him, of going to many race meetings.

However, she followed what was happening on the turf by reading the newspapers.

The Marquis found that this was so different from most women, who were only interested in going to Ascot or one of the Classic meetings where they were far more concerned with what they were wearing than with what the horses were doing.

"I would love to own a racehorse," Velina sighed wistfully.

It was with difficulty that he just prevented himself from telling her that he possessed a number of them and they had won quite a few Classic races.

"Now what you must do," he said as they finished their meal, "is to go to bed and sleep peacefully. I will call you early and we should set off as quickly as possible."

He thought that she looked surprised and explained,

"It is always best to ride in the cool of the day. If it gets much hotter, we may have to rest the horses when the sun is blazing."

"Of course we will," Velina agreed. "But I would not have thought of it if I had not been with you."

She paused for a moment before she went on,

"Thank you! Thank you for being so very kind and so understanding. When we reach Yorkshire, I know that my aunt will thank you, too."

"That is some way ahead. Now as I have already said that I think it is time for bed."

She smiled at the Marquis.

Then she walked up the stairs and he was aware, as she did so, that she had an exquisite figure and she moved with an elegant grace that he appreciated. So many young girls, especially *debutantes*, were clumsy and rather rough in their movements.

He felt as if Velina was almost flying up the stairs, her feet hardly touching the steps.

She reached her room and stood still for a moment until the Marquis joined her.

Then she said,

"Goodnight! And thank you again, Neil."

"Thank me when we get safely to where you want to go," the Marquis replied. "In the meantime I should be thanking you, because I have enjoyed your company when I thought that I would be entirely on my own."

"Good night and God bless you," Velina said as she closed the door of her room.

It was a long time, he thought, since anyone had said 'God bless you!' to him.

He remembered that his mother had said it, also his Nanny, but then the women he had slept with had seldom referred to God.

He was just about to undress when he thought it wise to take a last look at the horses to make sure that they did not need anything or perhaps they had been joined by newcomers and there was indeed plenty of room for them.

He was always afraid that, because his horses were outstanding and so different from those ordinary men rode, that they might be stolen.

He therefore went quietly down the stairs and let himself out by the back door that led into the courtyard.

There was no one to be seen and, when he walked into the stable, he found that both horses were lying down, and so he did not disturb them, but merely made sure that there was water in buckets and food in the manger.

Then, just as he turned to leave the stable, a cart carrying three men and drawn by two horses, clattered into the stable yard.

As he did not want to be seen, he moved back into the doorway.

Two of the men then clambered out of the cart and walked into the inn, while the third man sat in the driving seat obviously waiting for them.

The Marquis stayed exactly where he was, thinking it a mistake to show himself.

He did not realise at that moment that they could be the men Velina was afraid might be following her.

The man in the cart lit a pipe and then the two men came out from the inn.

The Marquis, who had left the door ajar, saw one of them go to talk to the man in the driving seat.

"I thinks we've found 'er," he heard the man say.

"You 'ave!" the other exclaimed.

"Well, I thinks so. But I'm just goin' to 'ave a look at the 'orses in the stable. So if you asks me, Fireball'll be there and then we can be certain."

The Marquis moved quickly to the other side of the stable, where there was straw and hay in the stalls.

He slipped behind the hay and, kneeling down, was now completely out of sight.

A few minutes later two men came in through the stable door and they moved at once to the stalls.

"That one there be Fireball right enough!" one of the men exclaimed.

Then another man answered him,

"Yes, I recognise the 'ead of that 'orse. But the old man inside said she be with her brother. I didn't know 'er 'ad one."

"Nor did his Nibs for that matter," the other replied. "If you asks me, she sent for 'im and slipped away, as we know, so that no one were aware of it until 'er be gone."

"That be a fine 'orse in the other stall," the man he was speaking to muttered. "If you asks me, if it ain't 'er brother, it be a man who can afford the best."

"We're not concerned with 'im," the first man said, "but with the girl. If we don't get 'er back to 'is Nibs, 'e'll be furious and won't pay us what 'e promised."

"Well, I can't drive no faster than we 'ave today," the other man said, "and, if we've now found 'er, let's 'ave somethin' to eat and drink before we takes 'er away."

"Now don't be stupid," the third man said. "We're not goin' to take 'er so that the man who owns this 'orse'll

62

make a scene. If 'e really is 'er brother, though I never knows she 'as one, 'e'll be within 'is rights."

"I didna think of that," the first man mumbled.

"Well think about it now. If 'e's 'er brother or 'er lover 'e won't be prepared to let 'er go back quietly wiv us. So we'll 'ave to steal 'er, so to speak."

"Steal 'er!" he exclaimed. "'Ow can we do that?"

"Well, we 'as to wait until everybody be asleep and then carry 'er out afore she makes a big fuss or attracts the attention of that there brother."

"'Ow do you know they ain't sleepin' together?"

"You 'eard what the old man told us. 'E said they took two rooms and seemed a very pleasant couple."

"All right! If you be certain it be 'er, tell us exactly what we 'as to do."

"What we 'as to do, boys, is to creep into 'er room. As I've done afore, so it'd better be me. As she be sleepin' I'll put somethin' over 'er mouth which'll prevent 'er from makin' a sound. Then we'll bring 'er down the stairs into the cart and drive orf."

"What about the 'orse?"

"We can come back for that later, if it's still there. Anyway we're not interested in 'orses, but in the money. That's what 'is Nibs promised us and that's what we'll get if we takes 'er back."

He paused before he continued,

"Now then you and me'll do that job. We'll pull the blanket off the bed, so she won't feel cold in the back of the cart as I don't suppose that she'll 'ave anythin' on but 'er nightgown."

"'Ow do you know all this?" one of them asked.

"Because I've done this sort of thing before," was the answer. "I got one woman out of prison when I were a soldier and no one knew she'd gorn until she were safely tucked up in 'er own bed."

"That were clever of you!"

"It were somethin' that paid well," the man replied. "But this one'll pay even better when we gets 'er back to 'is Nibs."

"We'll do exactly what you tells us" the other two said in unison.

"You'll be wantin' somethin' 'ard in your 'and just in case 'er brother wakes up and gets nasty," was the reply. "'E won't be armed and, if you knock 'im down with the first blow, 'e'll be unconscious until we're well on the way 'ome."

"I'll see to that. I'm goin' to get somethin' to eat. But I thinks it'll be a mistake to put the 'orses away just in case we 'as to move quickly. Not that I thinks that old'un and his wife'll be strong enough to stop a flea."

He walked out of the stable as he spoke and across to the man who was sitting with the horses.

The Marquis did not move an inch until he thought that they would have gone inside.

In fact, when he did move quietly towards the door, he saw that their horses had been attached to the pump in the centre of the yard and that food bags had been put over their noses.

He let himself out of the stable door and then very quietly opened the door into the inn.

Now he could hear all three men talking together in the dining room.

Slipping off his black riding boots that he had dined in, he walked silently up the stairs.

He was very careful as he did so not to attract the attention of the publican, who was in the bar, or his wife, who was in the kitchen.

He had said they would leave early and he knew that early to them would mean perhaps six or half-past at best.

He therefore thought it would be wise to give both Velina and the horses a rest before they escaped from the clutches of her enemies.

He undressed and climbed into his Spartan bed.

He left the door open so that if they tried to kidnap Velina earlier than he expected he would hear them before they opened her door.

Because he had been in the Army, he had learnt not only to wake early but at the exact time he wanted to.

But to make sure he would not oversleep, he drew back the curtains and pulled up the blind so that the first rays of sun would undoubtedly wake him.

Then, although it would seem somewhat strange to anyone else, he fell asleep.

Just as Velina and their horses were sleeping too.

*

He must have slept for four hours before he woke.

He was aware that the stars were just beginning to fade in the sky and he looked at his watch and saw that it was four o'clock.

He was quite certain that the men who were there to kidnap Velina would not consider the roads very safe while it was still dark.

He dressed himself rapidly

Going downstairs very quietly, he passed the dining room door.

As there were no more rooms in the inn, the men were lying on the floor with blankets and cushions and one of them, at any rate, was snoring loudly.

The Marquis saw that their horses were still tied to the pump, but their bags had been taken from their noses.

He crossed the yard and woke up both Fireball and Samson. He gave them a good rub down and saddled and bridled them.

Then he left them while he went back for Velina and walked up the stairs.

He went into her room very quietly and found as he expected that she was fast asleep. She, too, had slept with the curtains drawn back.

From the faint light coming through the window, he could see that her eyes were closed and her fair hair was falling, very attractively, over her shoulders.

He bent over her and whispered,

"Wake up! There is danger!"

Just for a moment Velina did not move.

Then her eyes opened and he whispered again.

"You are in danger! Get dressed quickly without saying a word. We have to leave at once!"

As he spoke, he put his finger against her lips and he knew that she understood him.

Then, as she started to climb sleepily out of bed, he went to his own room and packed up his belongings. He then put on his riding boots, which he had not done when he crossed to the stable.

When he returned to Velina, he found that she was already dressed except that her hair was still hanging over either side of her face.

"Come along," he muttered very quietly, "and don't make a sound!"

He then took her by the hand and drew her down the stairs.

She must have heard the men snoring in the dining room as they passed it.

The Marquis paused to put several sovereigns onto the table in the empty kitchen.

Taking Velina's hand again he drew her out into the yard and across it to the stable and she saw that the two saddled and bridled horses were waiting for them.

She did not speak as the Marquis lifted her up onto Fireball's back.

As she rode into the stable yard, he jumped onto Samson and followed her. There was no hiding the sound of the horses' hoofs on the cobbled yard.

Now the Marquis was moving Samson quickly and in fact he rode as fast as the stallion could manage down the lane and into the main road.

Then they were galloping through the village until they were out once again in the countryside.

Only then did the Marquis pull in his reins and take Samson down to a trot.

Velina did the same.

"What happened?" she asked. "Who were they and how did you know that they had come for me?"

"I was lucky enough to hear them when they came to the inn, saying how they intended to spirit you away."

"Oh, you have saved me!" Velina cried. "How can I thank you for doing anything so wonderful?"

"I think it was just chance they stopped there," the Marquis replied. "Then they saw Fireball and knew that they had found you."

"But we have escaped," Velina said, "you are quite certain that we really have got away from them?"

"I think we have made a good start on them. But we know that they are following us and I think we would be wise to make our way North by the side roads, which might easily put them ahead of us, but that, of course, is immaterial."

"I think you are brilliant!" Velina exclaimed. "I don't know how to begin to tell you how grateful I am."

"You must keep all that until we arrive safely," the Marquis answered. "But we must keep ahead of them if we can and make sure before you reach your aunt that she is not prepared to give you up to them."

"I am quite certain that Aunt Cecily will do nothing of the sort," Velina said. "But they might overpower her even though she has quite a large household."

"We will fight that battle when we come to it," the Marquis added. "But now I want to leave this road and go to Yorkshire by another route."

He did not wait for Velina to answer. He just turned round at the next cross roads.

He vaguely remembered that there were a number of different ways of reaching the North, but, when he was driving, he had always kept to the main roads because they were easier for his horses.

Now he told himself there was nothing to prevent them from riding over the land, which was certainly safer than the roads.

In future he would need to be much more careful in choosing where they slept.

He admitted to himself that it would be stupid if she was being followed, to stay anywhere on the main road.

He had in fact thought it unlikely that her stepfather would send these rough men to actually kidnap her rather than ask her politely if she would return home with them.

She must, he reckoned to himself, be part of a very strange family.

Or perhaps there were other more sinister reasons why her stepfather was so anxious for her to marry a man she disliked and feared.

'If the Duke does not think this is an adventure,' the Marquis thought to himself, 'then I am certain that neither he nor Alfred could find a better one.'

CHAPTER FOUR

The Marquis and Velina rode along a great many small narrow lanes that twisted and turned continually.

He guessed, as he had a good sense of direction, that they were moving North all the time.

They passed through a number of villages until they found one with a nice-looking black and white inn on the village green. It was much the same as the one they had stayed in the night before.

As they were alone in a small room, which was called the dining room and no one could hear them, Velina exclaimed,

"You were so wonderful, Neil, in getting me away from those men! I was terrified when you told me what was happening."

"They sounded particularly rough and uncouth," the Marquis said. "Why should your stepfather employ such people?"

"I expect they were men who were working in the fields. There have been a number of very strange workers at home since the war was over, when so many men were killed. The farmers, as they are so desperate, are prepared to take on anyone who has a pair of hands."

The Marquis knew this to be true.

But it told him that her stepfather had an estate, although he was not prepared to ask whether it was small or large and, because he had no wish to talk about himself, he was careful not to sound too inquisitive.

At the same time, because she was so beautiful, he was curious to find out more about her.

It certainly seemed strange that any man whom one could call a gentleman should employ such rough common men to find his stepdaughter.

The more he talked to Velina the more he became convinced that she was a lady from the top of her head to the soles of her feet.

Her manners were perfect and the way she spoke was without a mispronounced word,

But she was obviously totally innocent of the world outside her home.

They were given a rather unimaginative but edible luncheon, which was usually provided by the inn and they both drank cider.

When they had finished, ending with cheese, which was surprisingly good, the Marquis suggested,

"I suppose we must get on. We still have a long way to go, as you well know, Velina."

"I keep thinking how lucky I am to be with you," she replied. "I know it was wrong to speak to a stranger, but I was so frightened that my stepfather would send men after me and, of course, as happened last night, if they had not recognised me, they would know Fireball."

"He is certainly a very good-looking horse and you are lucky to have him. I am sure that he and Samson will survive this long and arduous journey better than we will."

"I am not so afraid of it now I am with you," Velina said. "Thank you again, Neil, for being so kind to me."

"You can thank me when I deliver you safely to your relative and that will not be for some time."

He rose from the table as he spoke and Velina did the same.

He was about to pay the publican when she said,

"Please, I ought to give you some money for my expenses. I did think about it this morning when we were leaving the inn, but we were in such a hurry to get away I did not like to delay things."

"We were lucky," the Marquis answered, "to have such a good start. I think that the best arrangement would be that if you do owe any money, which I think is unlikely, we add it all up when you are safely at your aunt's home."

Velina smiled at him.

"I am so very very lucky to have found you and I think it was because I prayed frantically as I left home. Apart from anything else, I really did not know the way."

"Well, we may easily make a mistake," the Marquis said, "considering all the twisting and turning that we have done already. So the sooner we set off now and find a quiet place to stay the night the better."

"We must make sure that those men don't find me," Velina murmured with a little shiver.

The Marquis did not answer.

He merely called the publican of the inn over and paid him for their luncheon.

He also asked him which was the quickest route to the main road North and he learnt that it was only a mile to their left and the road connecting to it was after they had passed the next village.

Listening to him, Velina thought that he was being very clever in making the publican, in case he was asked, think that they were taking the easiest way North.

When they went outside and collected their horses, Velina said as they rode off,

"Now we know we are going in the right direction. But I think the men will be hurrying as fast as they can on the road we are avoiding. They would not wish to admit to my stepfather that they found me and then lost me again."

"I think that we are doing the right thing and you are not to worry about it," the Marquis replied. "Just leave it to me and try to enjoy the sunshine and forget that there are three unpleasant-looking creatures searching for you."

"I will try," she answered, "but I am so petrified of having to go back."

"We will avoid that if nothing else," the Marquis assured her. "Leave it in my hands, which I promise you, are very capable."

"I think you are so marvellous," Velina murmured. "Every time I think about it, I say a prayer of thankfulness that I was brave enough to speak to you."

"I suppose it did not strike you that, as I was just a stranger, I might have taken you back to your stepfather, believing that he would pay me for doing so?"

"I did not think of that at the time," Velina replied, "but I did notice the horse you were riding and thought that only a man who loved and understood horses would own such a fine specimen."

The Marquis thought that this was an astute answer.

As they rode on, he continued to talk to Velina, not about personal matters, as he knew that they would be embarrassing, but of the history of the County they were riding through.

This led, as some of the houses were Elizabethan, into the history of England itself.

He learnt, as he expected, that she was extremely well educated. Combined with her beauty and the horse she was riding, he was certain that her family were well off and well bred.

Because he spoke to her very skilfully, extracting interesting information from her without her being aware of it, he found it one of the more amusing conversations he had ever taken part in.

Before, when he had been with a beautiful woman, she had insisted on talking about love and their feelings for each other.

Velina spoke completely impersonally and it told him that she had never learnt how to flirt with a man. In fact she had no idea of how to do so.

*

They had ridden for nearly an hour when they came to a very pretty little village.

The cottages had thatched roofs and small gardens, which were filled with flowers and everything seemed very spick and span.

There were few people to be seen at the early part of the afternoon and Velina knew that this would mean that the men were out at work, whilst the women were resting before they fetched their children from the school.

It was then she became aware that one of the packs hanging from Samson's saddle had come loose at one end.

She pointed this out to the Marquis, saying,

"Don't move! I know what has happened and I will put it right. Otherwise Samson will find it banging against him all the time."

Before the Marquis could protest that he would do it himself, she had dismounted from Fireball, handed him her reins to hold and went to the side of Samson.

"It's not broken," she told him. "It has only come undone as you could not have tied it on as tightly as you should have done."

The Marquis thought that it was something he was not used to doing himself and therefore it was not at all surprising that he had made a mess of it.

But he did not say so. He only thought how agile Velina was in the way she moved and the quickness of her fingers.

Then, as she tied the pack tightly so that it would not fall again, there was a sudden yelping of a dog from the cottage near where they were standing.

A small dog, still yelping loudly, came rushing out through the open door.

It was obviously in pain and the man following it had a whip in his hand.

"You get out of 'ere and stay out, you varmint!" he shouted in a thick voice, which made the Marquis aware that he had had too much to drink.

Then, as the man struck the dog again, it squealed as it ran down the path to the gate.

A small boy came running after it, crying,

"You're not to 'it 'im! You're not to 'it Jimmie."

"I'll 'it 'im and I'll 'it you 'ard if I 'as any more nonsense from either of you," the man screeched.

As he spoke he raised his whip and brought it down hard on the boy's shoulders.

He screamed and the man hit him again.

This time the boy fell over onto the ground.

Then the man went back into the house, staggering drunkenly as he did so.

He slammed the door shut and they heard the sound of him locking it.

Almost before the Marquis realised exactly what was happening, Velina had leapt from Samson's side.

Opening the garden gate, she was crouching down and putting her arms round the boy.

He was sobbing from the dreadful violence that had been unleashed on him and the dog was whimpering.

Velina held the boy close.

"It's all right," she said soothingly. "He will not hurt you anymore."

"I want me Mum!" the boy sobbed. "I want 'er!"

"Where is your mother?" Velina enquired.

She was holding the boy in her arms as she spoke and he was still crying against her shoulder.

The Marquis was aware that a woman had come out of the cottage next door, having heard the noise, and was now looking over her hedge.

"Who is that man," the Marquis asked, "who is so cruel to this small boy."

"That be 'is uncle," the woman answered, "and a nasty piece of work 'e is too! He drinks 'imself silly and then takes it out on that small child."

"It's a disgrace!" The Marquis was now frowning. "Something should be done about it."

The woman did not answer and after a moment he asked,

"Where are his mother and father?"

"'Is father be killed in the war and 'is mother be attendin' the death of her father who lived at Fairfield."

"Then the best thing we can do," the Marquis said, "is to take the boy to her. He can hardly stay with a man who is as cruel as that."

"'E be real wicked to that poor child and 'is dog," the woman said. "But there ain't nothin' we can do."

"Surely you have a Vicar in this village?"

The woman shook her head.

"No, we shares 'im with three other villages and 'e's only able to come 'ere three times a month."

The Marquis knew that this had been another thing which had happened since the war when there were not so many people willing to pay the Vicar's stipend as there had been in the past.

He therefore said to the woman,

"Would you be kind enough to hold these horses for a moment, while I see what I can do about that little boy and his dog."

The woman looked surprised.

"There be nothin' you can do," she said. "If 'e's locked them out they'll not get into the 'ouse till it's dark."

The Marquis thought that he would like to give that man some of his own medicine, but he thought it would be a mistake, as Velina was with him, to make a scene.

"Now tell me exactly where the child's mother is staying," he said to the woman.

"It be at Fairfield which be two mile up the road," she replied.

"And her name?"

"Mrs. Slater."

The Marquis did not wait for more and he passed through the gate into the garden towards Velina.

The boy was crying a little less now, but still there was a sob on his breath.

Velina was still holding the boy close to her and the dog was rubbing his nose against her knee.

She had pulled off her hat so that she could look after the boy more easily.

The Marquis thought, with her hair shining in the sun, it made a very touching picture and one that he would like to have painted.

He bent down and said,

"What I am going to suggest is that we now take this boy to his mother. She lives only a little way up the road and I am sure that she would not like him treated in this cruel manner."

"Can we really do that?" Velina asked.

She looked up at him with such an expression of admiration in her eyes that the Marquis thought no woman could ever look more grateful, even if he had given her a necklace of diamonds.

He picked the boy up in his arms and urged,

"Come along young man. I am now going to take you riding on my horse to find your mother."

The boy gave a little cry of delight.

Then he said,

"I can't leave Jimmie."

"No, of course not, we will take him too and I am sure that your mother will be pleased to see you both."

He carried him in his arms out of the garden and placed him on Samson's back. Despite the fact that he had been cruelly hurt, the boy was so thrilled at being on such a large horse that he stopped crying.

He sat still staring at Samson's head as if he could hardly believe what was happening.

Velina picked up the dog, which was quite a small mongrel, and she could well understand that, to the boy, he was something precious and perhaps the only thing he had to love in a house of cruelty.

The woman from the house next door was looking with astonishment at what was happening.

"You'll find Mrs. Slater in the second cottage on the right when you comes into the village," she said. "'Er father were a very respected man and were the Verger in the village until 'e became too old."

"Thank you for helping us," the Marquis replied. "I am sure that Mrs. Slater will thank you when she comes back. Although perhaps she will be able to stay where she is and keep the boy with her."

The woman shook her head.

"No! Now her father be dead they 'as to give up the 'ouse which they lets 'im keep because 'e was so old and 'ad been a long time at the Church. I understands from Mrs. Slater afore she went away that there be another man waitin' to go into it now 'er father's passed on."

The woman was obviously glad to impart all this information and the Marquis thought she was undoubtedly the village gossip.

That he and Velina were now taking the boy would certainly be passed from cottage to cottage after they left.

The Marquis, having learnt all that he needed to know, turned to help Velina.

She managed with extreme dexterity, he thought, to climb onto Fireball without any help.

Then he handed her the dog which she put in front of her and then he climbed up onto Samson, aware that the small boy was very excited at riding anything so large.

The Marquis managed, however, to raise his hat to the woman who had been talking to him and, as he rode off, he thought that she would have enough to gossip about for at least a week.

Then, as they moved out of the village, the Marquis said to the boy who was sitting firmly, as if entranced, in front of him,

"Now tell me your name."

"Me Mum always calls me Johnny," he said. "But at school I be just John."

"Well, I think that Johnny and Jimmie are both very nice names," the Marquis answered.

The boy turned to look at his dog.

"I think Jimmie likes ridin' on a big 'orse – like I am," he said.

He had obviously by now forgotten how cruelly he had been struck by his uncle.

But the Marquis was aware that there were marks on his neck that had obviously been inflicted on another occasion as well as on the lower part of his arms, which were not covered by the woolly jumper he was wearing.

The Marquis glanced at Velina riding beside him.

By the smile on her lips and the light in her eyes, he knew how pleased she was that he was helping the boy.

"How long has your mother been away?" he asked Johnny.

"A long, long time!" the boy replied, "and Uncle Simon beat me every night when I fed Jimmie because 'e was 'ungry or because he 'id in my bedroom."

He glanced at Velina as the boy was talking and he saw by the expression in her eyes how angry it made her.

"Will your mother have to go back to the house you have just left," she asked quietly.

"We've nowhere else to go. It be Uncle Simon's 'ouse and 'e 'ates us livin' there with 'im."

"What happened to your father?" Velina asked him, almost knowing the answer before the boy replied,

"Dada very brave. He be killed in the War fightin' those wicked Frenchmen."

It was what she had expected and she glanced at the Marquis, who said,

"I feel sure that we will find a better place for your mother and you."

Johnny, however, was not actually paying attention.

He merely asked,

"Make big 'orse go faster, please! I want to ride very very fast."

They had been walking down the road, but now the Marquis put Samson into a trot and Velina did the same with Fireball.

It was rather difficult riding with only one hand and she had to hold the dog very close to her.

She was not certain if she put it down onto the ground whether it would follow them.

"Are you all right, Velina?" the Marquis enquired.

"So far so good. It was brilliant of you to find out if we could take the boy to his mother. I was feeling desperate at leaving him with that horrible cruel man."

The Marquis thought that it would be a mistake to say too much in front of the child.

But Johnny was not listening.

"Faster! Faster!" he cried.

To please him the Marquis moved at a very fast trot down the road with Velina keeping up behind.

She thought, as she did so, how kind he was and how lucky she was to find someone so understanding.

'First of all he had to save me,' she mused, 'and then Johnnie. He really is a remarkable person.'

However she had to spend her time keeping Jimmie from slipping off her saddle and she was glad when the Marquis turned right and she realised that they were now in Fairfield village.

There were not many cottages and it was easy to find the second one on the right which the Marquis realised was a little larger than the ordinary village cottages.

He was wondering what Velina would say if the child had to go back with his mother to the house they had just left.

There was no one to be seen in the small garden that stood in front of the house and so he dismounted and left Johnny sitting on the saddle.

"Now hold the reins tightly," he said, "and don't let Samson move until I come back."

He had an idea that he might want to ride off on his own and he glanced at Velina as he spoke who understood.

The Marquis opened the garden gate and walked up the narrow path towards the front door.

Even as he did so, he thought the house somehow looked empty and, when he knocked on the door, there was no reply.

He knocked again and then thought that he would walk round the back in case Johnny's mother was in the kitchen and had not heard him.

There was a narrow path taking him to the back of the house, where there was another garden, but he noticed that it was un-weeded and there were few flowers.

The kitchen door was also closed and he was just wondering what he should do when he saw a woman come out of the next-door cottage.

She was beginning to hang out the clothes that she had washed on the line.

He went to the side of the garden and said,

"Forgive me for bothering you, madam, but where is Mrs. Slater, who I understand was staying in this house."

The woman looked round in surprise and then took a clothes peg out of her mouth before she replied,

"She were buried this mornin'!"

"Mrs. Slater?" the Marquis questioned. "I thought it was her father who had died."

"Oh, 'e died just last week and 'er catches the same disease as 'e 'ad!" the woman replied. "I don't know what it's called, but it be very dangerous. When she died a few days ago, they buried her ever so quick, in case any of us got it."

She spoke almost indignantly as if it was annoying of her neighbour to have been so ill.

"So Mrs. Slater is dead!" the Marquis said as if he was confirming it to himself.

"Yes, 'er died and the Vicar says as to 'ow 'e'd tell 'er son, but he weren't going to Merrycroft till tomorrow."

The Marquis realised that no one in Merrycroft, if that was the name of the village that they had just left, was aware of the tragedy that had overcome Mrs. Slater when she had gone to bury her father. In fact it was doubtful if even her drunken brother was aware of it.

He saw that the woman who had been speaking to him was staring at him as if surprised at his appearance.

Then she said,

"If you be wantin' to go into their 'ouse I thinks, being as 'ow they both died of some nasty disease, it'd be a stupid thing to do. That's what I and the other people in the village thinks."

The Marquis thought that it would be a mistake for him to do so even if it was possible.

So he thanked the woman with the washing for her information and, raising his hat politely, he walked away.

When he went back to where Velina was waiting for him, he heard Johnny talking excitedly about Samson.

"I think 'e could go faster than any other 'orse I've ever seen," Johnny was saying, "and I'd like to ride 'im in a race. I knows 'e'd come first."

"I am sure he would," Velina answered, "and when you are older you shall ride a horse as big as Samson and perhaps win a very big race."

As she then saw the Marquis coming through the gate, she asked him in a very different voice,

"What has happened?"

"I will tell you, but I think that we should move away from here," he said.

He was not only thinking that the house might be infectious from the disease, but thought it a mistake to let the woman next door see Johnny as it would be a story that would go round the village before nightfall.

He therefore mounted Samson and they rode on.

Although Velina looked at him in a puzzled way, he said nothing.

In fact the Marquis did not speak until they were well out of the village.

Then he said, in French, wondering if Velina would understand,

"The child's mother is dead. I would suppose that the only thing we can do is to take him back to his uncle."

He was not surprised when Velina answered him in the same language,

"In that case he will be alone with that terrible man. Oh, please, please we cannot do that!"

"Then what do you suggest we do?" he asked still in French.

Velina was silent for a moment.

Then she said,

"I am sure my Aunt Cecily would know someone on her estate who would take him in. There are always people who long for a child who are unable to have them."

The Marquis knew this to be true.

And he was certain that there was someone on his own estate who would be only too willing to take such a nice little boy and his dog into their care, especially if he paid them to do so.

At the same time he could not, at the moment, talk of his own affairs until he had won the Duke's bet.

So they were now saddled with Johnny and his dog unless they handed him over to a man who would beat him, perhaps even more cruelly than he had done already.

He was then aware that, riding beside him, Velina was thinking and perhaps praying for some solution.

Finally with a twist of his lips the Marquis said,

"Well, since I seem to have adopted you, I suppose the only thing I can do is to adopt Johnny too and take him with us on our long journey to the North."

Velina looked at him.

"Do you really mean that?" she asked.

"I cannot think of any other solution unless I hand him over to the Police, who will undoubtedly take him to his nearest relative, who is his uncle."

"Please let him – stay with us," Velina pleaded, "I will look after him and, although it might make us a little slower, I am sure he will do exactly what we want him to do. Please – please say yes, Neil!"

The Marquis smiled.

"I really don't seem to have much choice," he said. "Having adopted a sister, I now have to adopt a child who will have to be another relation of some sort!"

He laughed because it all sounded so ridiculous.

He thought that even the Duke would be impressed by this turn of Fate.

"Oh, thank you! Thank you!" Velina exclaimed. "I could not have slept if we had returned him to that awful man. I would have gone back and taken him with me."

"I am sure that the man your stepfather wanted you to marry would have been pleased if you had arrived with a child, who, of course, you might tell him is your own!"

Velina grinned.

"I had not thought of that. It would certainly be a surprise. But actually I think that Johnny is too old for me to say he is mine."

"We will soon find out," the Marquis said. "Tell me Johnny, how old are you?"

Johnny, who was concentrating on Samson, did not answer for a moment and then he replied,

"Me Mum said I was seven on my last birthday and she gave me seven bars of chocolate."

"That was a very nice present," the Marquis said. "I am sure you are a very sensible boy for your age."

"Me Mum says I'm very good," Johnny answered, "and I 'elp 'er when she's doin' the washin' and I clean the kitchen."

Suddenly he turned his head and said,

"We're out of this village now, I thought me Mum was stayin' 'ere 'cos Grandpapa was dead."

The Marquis drew in his breath.

"I am afraid that your mother has gone away and therefore, Johnny, we have to ride on to find her."

Johnny smiled.

"I like ridin' big 'orse, sir."

"So have you ridden a horse before?"

Johnny nodded.

"A boy at school 'ad a pony and 'e was kind to let me ride it lots of times."

The Marquis knew this was the answer he wanted.

When they had gone on a little further, they entered another village and at once he saw a shop at the side of the road and drew in his horse.

"You stay here in the saddle!" he ordered Johnny. "Hold on to the reins and make Samson wait for me."

Johnny was delighted.

"I'll do that, sir."

"If you are wise you will pat him gently with one hand and talk to him," the Marquis said. "Horses like to be talked to and it keeps them quiet."

Velina wondered why he was going into the shop, which looked to her a very typical village shop that sold everything.

The Marquis was not away for long.

When he came back, he handed Johnny a large bag of sweets, which made him give a whoop of joy.

Before he mounted Samson he went to the other side of Fireball and said to Velina,

"If he is to join us, I must find him something to ride. I am told that there is a farmer, who farms about half-a-mile from here, with a pony for sale."

"You would buy it for Johnny?" she asked.

"He will be more comfortable and so will I," the Marquis replied, "although it will undoubtedly make us slower than we wanted to be."

Velina smiled.

"I am not in a hurry and if you want to go away you must, of course, do so and leave him with me."

"I think as things are," the Marquis said, "you need someone to look after you just as you want to look after Johnny. Therefore we had better stay as we are. At the same time I am wondering just how large my family will be before I reach Northumberland!"

"You are too kind!" Velina whispered. "I will pay for Johnny."

"I have already told you we will argue about money when we reach our destination. So come along and let's hope the pony is properly trained otherwise we might have Johnny with us on a stretcher."

Velina gave a cry of horror.

"You are frightening me. I am sure that he is a very sensible boy and will do exactly what you tell him."

"I only hope that you are right, but he is certainly an attractive little chap and I am sure when we do reach your aunt's that either you or I will find someone who will care for him as he is so bereft of people at the moment."

Velina bent down to whisper in his ear,

"And I should not tell him about his mother at the moment, as it will only make him unhappy."

"I agree that it would be a mistake," the Marquis answered.

He thought as Velina bent towards him to whisper in his ear that there was a faint scent of violets that came from her hair.

As they rode on, he thought that, if she could afford an expensive scent and was continually offering to share expenses with him, she was not penniless.

It was another piece of information he could add to what he knew about Velina, which was still very little.

Equally it was all a puzzle that he found extremely interesting and unusual and it was definitely something he would add to the story he was planning to tell the Duke.

They rode on and came to the farm.

It was then that Velina turned to the Marquis and said to him in French,

"I think that you should go ahead and find out first if the pony is available and if it is well-trained. If Johnny sees it and thinks that you are going to give it to him, he will be so excited it will only upset him if you decide after seeing it, it is not good enough."

"I know exactly what you are saying," the Marquis agreed, "and I will do just as you suggest. You and Johnny stay here and let the horses eat the grass. I am sure it will do Jimmie good to have a run with his young Master."

Velina smiled at him.

"You are very sensible," she said. "I feel that you must already have a family of your own. Although I am curious, I have not yet asked you if you are married."

"I am not married," he replied, "and therefore, at the moment, have no children. But I am hoping that one day I will have a sporting little boy who enjoys riding as much as Johnny does."

"I am sure you will and it is what I want myself," Velina said.

There was a note in her voice that told the Marquis, without words, that she was thinking again of the man her stepfather was forcing her into marring and how terrible it would be if she had a child by him.

Then he told himself how ridiculous he was being.

Putting Johnny down onto the ground, he then rode off to leave them in a corner of a field where the horses found plenty to eat.

Velina sat under a tree which was a protection from the sun and Johnny sat down beside her.

"When I am big," he said, "I'm goin' to 'ave lots of 'orses just like these and they'll run ever so fast and we'll win lots of races."

"If you make up your mind and put that in your prayers, I am sure it will happen," Velina told him.

"Me Mum said I 'ad to pray to be a good boy and do as I was told," Johnny said.

"Quite right," Velina agreed, "and that is what you must do! At the same time God will always hear when you ask for something special and, if you have horses of your own, you will have to learn about them."

She smiled at him before she went on,

"You will have to take good care of them and talk to them, like the kind man told you to do just now."

Johnny thought this over for a while and then, with his head on one side, he said,

"If I talk to the 'orses, will they talk back to me?"

"They will in a way. I talk to Fireball and tell him he is a good boy and that he must jump the next fence with plenty of room to spare. Then he does what I tell him."

She paused before she added,

"When I tell him how fast he can go, he obeys me, just as he obeys me when I tell him to stop and not to push forward as he wants to do."

"I will talk to my 'orse like that when I 'ave one," Johnny said.

They were still discussing horses when a little later they saw the Marquis coming back towards them

Velina jumped up and ran to him first.

"Was it any good?" she asked.

"The pony was too slow and too old," the Marquis replied. "But he has a yearling there that I think Johnny will be able to manage."

"A yearling?" Velina questioned.

"He is young, but he has already had quite a lot of training," the Marquis said. "The farmer has a son of his own who is fifteen and who has been riding him for six months. But the horse is now too small for him."

Velina looked at Johnny talking to Fireball.

"I only hope we don't have an accident," she said. "It would certainly make us very slow if we had to keep to the speed of an old tired pony."

"That is what I was thinking," the Marquis replied. "It would also be very uncomfortable both for Johnny and me to share the same saddle."

Velina laughed.

"That is the real reason why you are buying the yearling!"

"You can hardly blame me for thinking of my own comfort," the Marquis replied. "What I have really come to tell you is that whilst the farmer is grooming the horse, which I have insisted on and finding a saddle I can buy, his wife invited us to tea. I am sure that is something Johnny will enjoy. So will you."

"You think of everything," Velina said. "And I am perfectly content to do whatever you suggest."

The Marquis felt that the expression of gratitude came from her heart.

At the same time, although she had no idea what it might have suggested, his eyes were twinkling.

CHAPTER FIVE

They took tea with the farmer and his wife and as the Marquis had expected, it was a substantial meal with eggs and meat for the men.

He thought that they would be in no hurry to reach a place to stay.

He asked the farmer if there was a good inn about ten or fifteen miles away.

"I knows of one," he said. "It be in a village called Hopely and I went there some years ago."

The Marquis thought that at least it was on the road they were already on, while the farmer's son was giving Johnny instructions how to handle the yearling and he was also telling him his name.

"I've always called 'im 'Hunter'," he explained, "as I was allowed, the first time I rode 'im, to go out with the 'ounds."

"I think it's a good name," the Marquis said, "as we have had to hunt for him and you have been kind enough to find him for us."

The farmer laughed at this, but his wife advised,

"You be very careful, young man. Them 'orses can be dangerous animals. If you rides 'im carefully and obey this kind man, you'll come to no 'arm."

"I'll do what 'e tells me," Johnny agreed as Velina smiled at him.

They set off at a fairly good pace.

From the farmer's description of it, the inn that they were seeking might be even further than the Marquis had expected.

Johnny was very excited at the idea of riding such a fine horse and the farmer's son gave him some last minute instructions when he was in the saddle.

Watching him, however, the Marquis realised that he was a natural horseman so that when he was older he would obviously be a very good rider.

He had often wondered why he himself had been able to ride so well when he was still very young and he was sure that it was an inheritance from his father who was an outstanding equestrian.

He had had friends when he had been at school who had no idea how to handle a horse and they always turned out to be bad riders.

This had convinced him that it was something one inherited in one's blood and was an excellent attribute to possess.

As Johnny rode a little ahead of him, he told Velina what he was thinking and she agreed with him.

"I always thought I inherited my love of horses and the way I can handle even the most difficult of them from my father," she said. "I believe that my grandfather was also a fine equestrian and much admired when he rode to hounds."

The Marquis longed to ask her who her father and grandfather were. But he knew if he did so he would have to say who he was and that would be a mistake.

They had introduced themselves at the beginning by their Christian names and that is how it should remain until the end of their journey.

However, he thought that every day he spent with Velina, he found her more and more interesting. She was so different in every way from the young women he had known before.

He realised soon after they met that she was very well read and, when he spoke of anything historical she was not only well aware of the facts, but often knew more than he knew himself.

As they rode along narrow lanes, he thought that no one could look more elegant or more attractive on a horse.

He was quite certain, from some of the things she had said to him that she had hunted with a major pack.

When they eventually arrived at the inn the farmer had recommended, Johnny was now obviously tired, but the Marquis, however, made him put his horse into the stall in the yard of the inn.

He was also told to see that there was food in the manger and fresh water in the bucket.

When he had done that, he told him to run and find Velina, while he saw to the two other horses.

Then he walked to the inn to join Velina.

He had asked when they had dismounted whether they could stay for the night and the publican had told him that it was possible and there was an enthusiastic note in his voice that told the Marquis that paying customers were few and far between in this isolated spot.

Velina was sitting alone by the fireplace and, as he sat down beside her, he enquired,

"Where is Johnny?"

"I showed him his room," Velina replied, "and told him to undress and get into bed. He is very tired and after such a large tea he is not hungry. But I have ordered some soup which I will take up to him when it is ready."

"I can see you are a very efficient Nanny besides everything else," the Marquis commented with a smile.

"He is a dear little boy and I don't think he will be any trouble to us," Velina replied. "But I have not yet told him that his mother is dead."

"He does not appear to miss her very much, and so I would keep the bad news until the end of our journey and then we will then have to find someone to adopt him."

"I don't think there will be any trouble about that, Neil. He is such a charming child that he deserves a kind and loving home."

"I am sure that you will be able to find one if I do not," the Marquis said.

"It was wonderful of you to find that horse for him, which is surprisingly quiet. When I saw him ride it, I just knew that there was no need to be nervous about him."

"I felt the same," the Marquis agreed. "I am just amazed that you should be so efficient when faced with a very unpleasant situation as we have had over Johnny."

"I don't wish to talk of that man who was so cruel to him," Velina said. "When I helped him off with his jacket, there was blood over the back of his shirt. I am wondering whether I could ask the publican's wife here to wash it before we start off tomorrow morning."

"I am sure she will do so if you are certain that it will dry in time," the Marquis replied.

"That is what is worrying me," Velina added.

Then suddenly she laughed.

"Why are you laughing?" the Marquis enquired.

"Because actually it is so funny," Velina answered. "Here we are fussing over a child we had not seen until this morning and all because I was brave enough to talk to you when I was escaping from my stepfather."

The Marquis laughed as well.

"It makes a story which might have come straight out of a book. It only remains for us to dig up gold in an unexpected place and that will make a significant finale!"

He thought as he spoke that the real end to the story was that he and Velina should fall in love with each other.

It was something he might have said laughingly to any woman he was flirting with or on the verge of having an *affaire de coeur*, but he realised from the first moment he met her that she was completely unaware of the world he lived in.

She had not once, as far as he could guess, looked upon him as an attractive man.

He had been friendly and he had helped her, but she talked to him as she might have talked to someone of twice his age or even to a trusted servant she had known since she was a child.

'If this is an experience for her,' he thought, 'it is also quite an experience for me and maybe a lesson I much needed.'

At that moment the publican's wife came in with a bowl of soup and said,

"Here's what you asked for and I 'opes the little'un enjoys it."

"I am sure he will," Velina replied, "and thank you very much for taking so much trouble."

She took the soup from the woman and walked to the stairs.

The Marquis took the liberty of asking what they were having for dinner and then suggested something extra that he thought Velina would enjoy.

"You must 'ave travelled a long way today," the publican's wife said curiously.

"We have indeed and your inn was recommended most favourably by a farmer," the Marquis told her, "and

He paused for a moment before he added,

"We don't often 'ave them as grand as that in this illage."

"Well, I am taking special care of them as you can understand," the Marquis said. "Thank you for the ent dinner and I hope to have a good sleep before we off tomorrow morning."

He ordered breakfast for eight o'clock and then upstairs.

There was no sound coming from Velina's room or the room next to it where Johnny was sleeping and he ght that they must be fast asleep after such a long day.

Then, as he opened Johnny's door to be quite sure he saw in the moonlight coming through the window he bed was empty.

The blankets were turned back and he thought that ust be with Velina.

At the same time the boy was clearly missing and, what he had just said downstairs, he felt anxious.

He went to the next room and was about to knock on door, but, as there was absolute silence, he then pushed en very quietly.

There was just enough light coming into the room him to be aware that Johnny was in bed with Velina.

He saw that Velina was asleep with her golden hair ing on either side of her face.

She had an arm round Johnny who was sleeping h his head on her shoulder.

Jimmie was sleeping comfortably at the end of the and, when he saw the Marquis, he wagged his tail but not make a sound.

For a moment the Marquis stood looking at them.

we were determined to reach you even though it was quite an effort."

"Well, we're right glad to 'ave you," the woman said, "and I 'opes you'll enjoy your dinner and 'ave a quiet night."

The Marquis assured her that they would and she went back to the kitchen.

It was some time before Velina returned and when she did the Marquis asked her,

"Is Johnny all right?"

"I have tucked him up in bed. He enjoyed the soup, but he was almost too sleepy to drink it."

"He is a very sporting little boy. We were lucky to find a horse he could ride."

"He will not be lucky if he has to be alone in the world," Velina said. "But I think his mother must have been very strange to have left him alone with that drunken uncle instead of taking him with her when she went to her father's funeral."

"I thought the same. It will mean that if he is not so fond of her as we expected, he will not be so upset when he learns that he will not see her again."

Velina gave a sigh.

"I cannot bear to think of him being unhappy. We must find a really nice couple to look after him, unless, of course, you adopt him yourself, Neil."

"I think that would be rather difficult," the Marquis replied. "One day I hope to have sons of my own who will enjoy riding as much as Johnny and you do."

And once again they were talking about horses.

When dinner was over, they continued to talk for some time until Velina asked,

"At what hour do you think we should leave here tomorrow morning?"

"There is no great hurry," the Marquis replied. "At the same time you want to put as many miles between you and your pursuers as is possible."

"Yes, of course," Velina agreed quickly. "Do you really think they will still be following me?"

"If your stepfather is determined to take you back," the Marquis replied, "presumably they will be looking for you further up the main road."

He saw Velina tremble and he added,

"Forget them for a moment. I am quite certain that they will not find us where we are now. I want you to look happy and not be frightened."

"But I am frightened. My stepfather, when he does make up his mind, can be so terrifying! He is absolutely determined I will marry this horrible man he has chosen for me."

"Do you think your aunt will be willing to protect you?" the Marquis asked.

"I know that she has never liked my stepfather and was devoted to my father. I can only hope for his sake that she will help me."

The Marquis was trying to remember exactly how powerful a Guardian could be and if there was any legal way that he could be removed from his position. However, he could not think of any solution to the problem.

After a moment's silence Velina rose to her feet.

"I am going to bed and I will be ready for breakfast at eight o'clock unless you would like it any earlier, Neil."

"No, eight o'clock will be fine for me," the Marquis replied. "Goodnight and sleep well."

Velina hesitated for a moment before saying,

"If by chance I am feeling frighte will call for you and then please come ai

The Marquis knew she was think men pursuing her could by chance find tl

"I am a light sleeper," he said rea only have to call out and I promise you tl you immediately."

"I thought it was what you would : you, thank you! There is so much I am vei for, I really don't know how to put it into

"Just take it for granted," the Marq think happy thoughts before you go to slee

"I will pray for you and Johnny," sl

Then, before the Marquis could rep the room and he heard her running up the s

He thought that there had been quite for one day and he hoped that there would b

However, he went to the stable to se were still there and he found all three of the which he thought he should be doing himsel

He locked the stable door and took publican.

"I hope you will understand," he said it to him, "that, as there are so many horse at the moment and my horses are very valuak happier if it is impossible for anyone to get in without making a noise."

The publican looked surprised.

"I never thinks of that," he said. "Bu you be right, sir. There be stories in the news day of somethin' bein' pilfered and it'd be a g for you to lose your fine 'orses."

He felt they created a picture that any great artist would be only too pleased to paint and then he closed the door very quietly and went to his own room.

It was some time before he fell asleep.

Because he was thinking of the picture Velina had made with Johnny, he wondered how many other people of his acquaintance would have taken an unknown small boy from a working class family into their arms.

He knew without being told that Johnny must have felt very alone and frightened.

Now the only world he had known with his mother and his cruel uncle had been left behind and this meant that everything that he was familiar with had been left behind as well.

It was a situation that he could understand himself,

But he most certainly did not think that the average woman, especially one who was obviously a lady by birth, would have understood the suffering of one small boy of no social standing and taken him into her arms.

'Velina is unique,' he thought to himself before he fell asleep.

*

The Marquis was woken because he heard Johnny talking in an excited voice to Velina.

He realised that they were both getting up in the next room, while he was still, as they thought, asleep.

He looked at his watch and saw that it was now a quarter-to-nine and he quickly jumped out of bed.

He was used to dressing himself very swiftly when he had to do so and after washing in cold water, he put on one of his clean shirts that Herbert had provided for him and walked through his door.

As he did so, he heard Johnny running downstairs.

Then he found that Velina's door was open.

She was packing her nightgown together with the other things she had needed into the one of the bags that was carried on Fireball's back.

She looked up at the Marquis and smiled.

"Good morning, Neil."

"Good morning," the Marquis answered. "I hope you slept well."

"Like a top and Johnny is in very high spirits. He is only afraid that the horse you bought for him yesterday is just a dream."

"The sooner we are on our way the better," he said. "I asked last night if breakfast could be ready at eight o'clock, but I overslept."

"I thought you would. I think that this has been the nicest place we have slept in."

"You are right," the Marquis agreed, "and certainly the food is better here than anywhere else."

By now Velina had finished packing the bag and the Marquis took it from her and carried it down the stairs.

A round table in the dining room was already laid for breakfast and Johnny was chattering to the publican's wife in the kitchen while Jimmie was having a large meal while he did so.

"A very good morning to you, sir," the publican's wife greeted him when she saw the Marquis.

"Good morning," the Marquis replied, "and thank you very much for your excellent dinner last night and I am certainly looking forward to my breakfast."

"It's ready for you now, sir, and I'll bring it straight in," she smiled.

Johnny slipped his hand into the Marquis's.

"She gave Jimmie an extra big dinner last night," he enthused, "and an even bigger breakfast this mornin'. He thinks this be a smashin' place and so do I."

"Well, you had better come and eat your breakfast," the Marquis told him, "because Hunter will be waiting for you outside."

They ate a large breakfast, the sausages being very delectable and the Marquis reflected that sitting round the table they looked a very homely family as anyone passing by would confirm.

He was thinking, however, that it was amusing that neither he nor Velina knew each other's full names.

Johnny, who any stranger would easily think that he was their son, was a boy they had just picked up while passing a cottage by the roadside.

"I was thinking that too," Velina said unexpectedly.

"Are you then reading my thoughts?" the Marquis asked.

"I can sometimes," she admitted. "In fact, I always knew what my father was thinking just as he felt the same about me."

"I found it happening abroad once in the East," the Marquis said. "But I have never met anyone who could do it in England."

"I will try not to be a nosey parker where you are concerned," Velina replied, "but sometimes I cannot help it!"

"I think it is a very dangerous activity. Suppose you were watching a man and reading his thoughts and realised that he was ready to rob a bank or even murder someone. Would you go to the Police?"

Velina put up her hands.

"Now you are trying to frighten me and I hope that will never happen. Although I can read your thoughts, it's not something I can do to everyone."

"Well, that is a relief at any rate, Velina. If my thoughts are very private, I will be annoyed if you not only read them but tell the world what I am thinking."

"Of course I would not do that," Velina answered. "Everything of yours is very special and secret because you have been so kind to me."

"I am pleased to hear that," the Marquis said. "The last person to read my thoughts was a very old Indian. As he had never been out of Bombay, my thoughts of England at any rate were quite safe."

Velina laughed.

"I am sure they were and anything I read I promise to keep to myself."

Johnny, who was giving little bits of his breakfast to Jimmie, was not listening to them.

Now having finished eating, he jumped up from his chair saying,

"Can I go and look at Hunter and ask him if he had a good sleep last night?"

"Of course you can," Velina replied. "You can put on his bridle, as I am going to dress Fireball as soon as I have finished my coffee."

Johnny hardly listened to her before he was out of the room and they heard him running across the yard with Jimmie at his heels.

The Marquis looked at Velina.

He felt that she looked even lovelier now than she had last night.

At the same time he thought that the picture of her and Johnny asleep in the bed at the inn would always be something he would remember.

Velina pushed her chair back.

"I am now going to get Fireball ready," she said, "as I am slower than you. But please don't forget that I will pay you back half the bill. So you must add to it what else I owe you."

The Marquis did not answer and she walked into the passage towards the door that led into the yard.

The Marquis went to the bar and, as he expected, he found the publican and paid his bill.

It was very reasonable considering all that they had had and the Marquis added a large tip.

The publican looked at it in surprise.

"You've given me too much," he queried.

"That is a present for your wife for being so kind and helpful," the Marquis told him. "You two must work very hard as I have not seen anyone else assisting you."

"I 'as a man who comes by three times a week to clean out the stables," the publican answered, "but the rest we does ourselves. It's 'ard to make enough money for the wife and me without 'avin' unnecessary expense."

"Well, we have been very comfortable here at your inn," the Marquis said, "and thank you very much."

"Thanks very much, sir. You be a real gentleman," the publican grinned, shaking him by the hand.

The Marquis felt that this was indeed high praise and he was smiling as he went into the kitchen to thank the publican's wife.

"It's been ever so nice 'aving you 'ere," she said, "and I 'opes you'll come again."

"I hope so, too," the Marquis replied.

He joined Velina to find that Johnny had put the bridle on Hunter correctly and it only remained for him to tighten the saddle.

"You have done very well, my boy," the Marquis praised him. "Now you must ride Hunter slowly to start with, otherwise you will get too far ahead of us."

"If we can go into a field, we can let 'im gallop," Johnny suggested.

"We have to find a field first, so take him slowly until we are clear of the village."

The other two horses were soon made ready and the Marquis then lifted Velina onto the saddle.

He picked up Jimmie and put him beside her.

"You take him for the first hour and I will take him for the second," he proposed.

"He is no trouble."

"A dog is always a trouble when he is on a horse," the Marquis replied. "But I think it's dangerous for him to run behind us when we are on the road. It's different when we are in the fields."

"Or if he was bigger," Velina said. "I am always afraid that if a small dog follows closely behind a horse he will be kicked."

She gave a little sigh before she added,

"The dog is all Johnny has of his own and whatever happens he must not lose Jimmie."

"You are quite right," the Marquis agreed. "So we must be very careful of him. We will take it in turns to have him and, when we find a field, we will have luncheon in the open air for a change. But I suppose I should have thought of that last night."

He did not say anything more, but hurried back into the kitchen.

It only took the publican's wife a short time to put together some cold chicken, slices of meat pie and a large piece of cheese.

She added chunks of newly baked bread and some butter and the Marquis then bought two bottles of cider and freshly made lemonade was put into a bottle for Johnny.

The parcel of food added a little to what Samson was already carrying and, when the Marquis joined Velina, she was smiling.

"It was clever of you to think of that," she said. "I wish I had thought about it myself. Of course Johnny will enjoy a picnic."

"Where is Johnny?" the Marquis asked.

"He has just ridden a little bit up the road and has promised me he will not go far," Velina answered.

The Marquis then hurried out of the yard and to his relief he saw Johnny about a quarter of a mile up the road.

When he and Velina joined him, Johnny piped up,

"I tried to hold Hunter back, but he said he wanted to gallop in the fields so you must not be angry with us."

"I am not angry," the Marquis told him. "But I was worrying about you and, of course, Hunter."

"We are all right," Johnny said, "and please can we ride really quickly?"

They rode on with Johnny riding ahead of them and the Marquis and Velina kept him well within sight.

Finally they came upon some open land, which was exactly what the Marquis was looking for.

"Now," he said to Johnny, "you can ride Hunter as fast as you like and we will follow you. But be careful of potholes."

Johnny had been waiting for this and he rode off at once with Velina watching him anxiously and the Marquis then said,

"He's all right! He is not going too fast and so the farmer was right when he claimed that the horse is well-trained."

"He is really too small to be riding a horse," Velina commented.

"I think he handles it as well as any boy of twelve or fourteen would do," the Marquis replied, "so you are not to worry."

She smiled at him.

"He is a dear little boy. As far as I can ascertain, no one loved him and his mother had not even taught him to say his prayers."

The Marquis looked at her, but he did not speak.

Then she continued,

"When I asked him if he had said his prayers, he replied, 'I only pray when I go to Church which isn't very often'."

"I am quite certain that you taught him a prayer," the Marquis said quietly.

Velina nodded.

"Yes, the one I always said myself when I was a child, and he knows now that not only God is listening to him but also his special angel up in Heaven."

The Marquis thought that this was what he would want his own children to learn when they were old enough to understand.

As they were both riding quickly to keep up with Johnny, he did not say anymore.

They rode on for the next two hours.

All the time Velina thought that they were getting further North and nearer to her aunt and that meant, she thought, when she reached her, her kind protector would say goodbye and then travel on to wherever he was going.

It then suddenly occurred to Velina that he had not explained why he was going North and she wondered if perhaps he had his family there.

He was so tall and such a good-looking man that she was sure he must have been pursued by quite a number of women.

She remembered her father being sarcastic about someone who lived near them.

He had been a very attractive man when he was young and her father had said that women in the County had run after him.

Velina wondered if Neil would think of her when they parted and if there would ever be any chance of them meeting again.

Then she told herself that she was asking too much.

She had been very very lucky in finding someone to escort her North and, of course, protect her from the men her stepfather had sent after her.

Even to think of them made her shudder and she wondered if she should ask Neil if there was anywhere she could go where she would not be found.

Then she thought it would be a mistake to be an encumbrance and she would just hope that her aunt would rally the rest of the family round her.

Then they could forcibly tell her stepfather that she could not be forced into marrying someone who she had no wish to marry.

It all seemed very simple.

At the same time she could not help thinking with a sinking heart that her aunt was not a very strong character and she might easily be trampled by her stepfather.

*

It was getting on for one o'clock when the Marquis saw ahead of them a great number of trees by the roadside and beyond them an open field.

The sun by this time was hot and he thought that they should have their meal with some protection from it.

He therefore called out to Johnny who was still well ahead of them and then they turned towards the trees.

"You must be tired of carrying that parcel," Velina said, "and I should have taken my turn with it."

The Marquis smiled.

"Are you suggesting that I am not strong enough to manage it?" he asked.

"Of course not, I only thought how uncomfortable it must be. It was so kind of you to think that it would be nice to sit in the shade and enjoy our luncheon."

"We have certainly not passed an inn that attracted me," the Marquis commented.

"I thought the same. I am certain that those kind people have provided us with something nice and edible."

"To make it a surprise, I will not tell you what there is," the Marquis joked.

Velina laughed.

"That makes it much more fun. Actually I have always enjoyed a picnic especially at Johnny's age."

"One person who will never go hungry is Johnny," the Marquis said, "and the other is Jimmie!"

"If we had tried to find a child and a dog who were amusing and really no trouble, we could not have done better."

"I agree with you. He is a delightful little boy."

"We must be very careful who we find to look after him," Velina remarked.

"I promise you that I will be very sure not to hand him over to anyone who would treat him as he has been treated in the past," the Marquis assured her.

There was a hard note in his voice that Velina did not miss.

She knew that Neil had been as horrified as she had been when the drunken man knocked the dog over and then poor little Johnny.

"I hate people who drink," she said almost speaking to herself.

"I hate them too, Velina. It is something that I will never do myself."

"I knew that before you told me," Velina answered.

Their eyes met and for a moment it was difficult to look away.

Then the Marquis said,

"We must stop under those trees. They are perfect cover for us and the horses. I know that we are going to enjoy our picnic."

"Yes, we will," Velina enthused.

They rode towards the trees.

She thought that the Marquis was undoubtedly the kindest and most charming man she had ever come across.

CHAPTER SIX

The publican's wife had provided a delicious picnic for them and Johnny was thrilled with it.

"Can I please have some more?" he asked, after he had eaten a mutton sandwich very quickly.

Velina laughed and gave him half of hers.

"I cannot have you starving yourself," the Marquis chuckled.

"I think a man's need is much more important than a woman's," she replied.

She knew that this it was an argument they would enjoy and as Johnny ate they talked, each trying to cap the others statement.

It was very quiet in the field that was empty of any animals and the only sound was birds singing in the trees above them.

"We have not too far to go now," the Marquis said. "In fact I think tonight will be the last time we will have to stay by the road before you reach your aunt."

It flashed through Velina's mind that that meant he would ride away and then she would never see him again.

She was about to protest when Johnny exclaimed, "Look!"

He pointed his finger at a man on a horse who was moving very swiftly towards them.

It occurred to Velina that perhaps it was the owner of the field and that they should not be trespassing.

As the horse came nearer to them, she gave a little gasp.

The man riding it had a black scarf pulled up over his chin and he also wore a mask over his eyes.

"It's a – highwayman!" she gasped.

The Marquis had been pouring lemonade out of a bottle and had not seen the horse approaching.

He looked up in astonishment.

Then the highwayman rode right up to them and he pointed at Samson with his gun.

"I'll take that 'orse!" he said in a harsh ugly voice, "and any money you 'ave in your pocket."

For a moment the Marquis stared at him.

Then he said to the highwayman,

"I think we can discuss this between us."

"I ain't discussin' nothin'," the man snarled at him. "You gives me the 'orse or I'll blow your brains out."

He was pointing his gun directly at the Marquis and Velina thought for a moment that there was nothing he could do.

Then she remembered that she had put in the side pocket of her riding jacket, a small pistol, which she had taken from her father's gun room before she ran away.

Because the weather had been so hot and she had always had her jacket undone she had hardly noticed that it was there and she thought that it would be safer there than in the bag on Fireball's saddle.

Quickly and without thinking, she pulled it out and shot at the highwayman.

He was looking at the Marquis and not at her and the bullet went into his arm and the vibration of the shot seemed to echo through the trees.

The highwayman gave a shout and almost fell off his horse.

As he did so, he very obviously had his finger on the trigger of his own gun and the shot went off into the air harmlessly.

It disturbed his horse which, after turning round, bucked furiously and started to gallop away.

As the highwayman was now very unsteady in the saddle when the horse bucked again, the man fell heavily to the ground.

It all happened so rapidly that Velina could only stare at the prostrate man, while his horse was galloping towards the other end of the field.

It was the Marquis who went into action swiftly.

He picked up Johnny and put him onto Hunter's back.

Then he turned towards Velina and picked her up.

As he did so, because she was so overcome at what had just occurred, she clung to him for a moment.

Bending his head he breathed,

"Thank you, darling," and kissed her.

Velina could hardly believe it was happening.

Then the Marquis lifted her gently onto the back of Fireball.

As she took the reins, he turned and then picked up Jimmie, who almost jumped onto Samson's back.

Then, as he called out, "follow me," he started to ride out of the field and back onto the road.

Velina and Johnny followed him obediently.

When they reached the road, they had to put their horses into a gallop to catch up with the Marquis.

They rode for at least a mile and a half at great speed and without speaking.

Then, as the Marquis began to ride a little slower, Velina moved Fireball beside him to ask in a whisper,

"Is he dead?"

The Marquis shook his head.

"No, your bullet hit him in the arm and he is now doubtless unconscious from the fall. But the last thing we want is anyone who heard the shot questioning us about what happened."

"Of course," Velina replied, "but it all took place so quickly."

"You were really superb," the Marquis smiled.

He looked at her as he spoke.

She was conscious that his lips had touched hers and, because it made her feel shy, she looked away at the road ahead.

Only when they had ridden a little further and the place where they had eaten luncheon was far behind them, did she feel as if the Marquis's lips were still pressing on hers.

It gave her a strange feeling that she had never had before.

She had never been kissed on the lips by a man.

It was something she had sometimes thought about and wondered what it would feel like.

Her father and his old friends always kissed her on the cheek as women did and when she kissed them back, she was usually aware of the roughness of their skin or the tickling feeling of their beards.

Now that the Marquis's lips had touched hers, she felt as if something strange was happening in her heart.

'He was just being grateful to me for saving him from losing Samson,' she told herself.

Yet she knew it was more than that.

It was something she had wondered about at night, but had evaded in the daytime.

Now she definitely knew, and there was no doubt about it, that she did not want to lose him.

When she reached her aunt's house in Yorkshire, he would doubtless say goodbye and continue on the journey he had arranged before she had asked to ride with him.

'If I lose him now,' she thought, 'I will never see him again. But it is doubtful if he will want to see me.'

She thought that she had never been so happy or so intrigued by anyone as she had been during these last few days when they had ridden together.

When they were not riding, they had then discussed every subject that was of interest to either of them.

If she was honest, Velina felt as if she had been in a dream.

Now she was convinced, with it all coming to an end that she would have to step back into reality.

The Marquis was now moving faster again and it was impossible to ask him any questions.

But two hours later when Johnny's horse seemed to be sagging a little and Velina thought that he must be tired, the Marquis asked if they wanted to stop.

"It's very hot," Velina replied, "and to tell the truth as we had not quite finished luncheon, I am rather thirsty."

"I'm thirsty too," Johnny chipped in. "I want some of that nice lemonade to drink."

"Then we will stop at the next inn," the Marquis promised. "I think now it is safe enough for us to do so."

He could see the question in Velina's eyes before she asked it.

"If the highwayman," he explained to her quietly, "is discovered before he has been able to move, there will be a great deal of excitement about it and the people in the village will be asking who shot him in the arm."

"Yes – of course," Velina sighed, "and they must not think it is us."

"They may indeed think so," the Marquis replied, "but we must not be available to give them an answer."

She now understood why they had ridden so far and so fast before resting.

"So you must be very careful," he said to Johnny, "what you say in front of people. If they think that we can give them any information about the highwayman, it might take a long time and we might have to appear at a Police enquiry."

"You are quite right, we must get away as far as we can, Neil." Velina agreed. "Perhaps we should go a few more miles before I quench my thirst."

"It's not as bad as all that," the Marquis answered, "but, if we go into the yard of an inn, we can drink without giving up our horses. I am sure we will find another place five or six miles away where we can stay the night."

Velina knew that he was being sensible about it and she was quite prepared to do anything he suggested.

They found a small roadside inn as he had expected three or four miles further on.

When they rode into the yard, there was a pump at which they could give the horses a drink.

Velina said that she would do it, while the Marquis went inside to find some lemonade for her and Johnny.

However, he ordered a somewhat stronger drink for himself.

No one knew better than he did that it would be a disaster for them to be concerned with the highwayman.

To begin with he would have found it difficult not to say who he was, which would have meant that, because of his title, the incident would be reported avidly in all the national newspapers.

Then there would be more explaining as to why he was accompanied by an extremely pretty girl and a young boy who did not belong to either of them.

He ruminated that anyone with a pencil and paper could write a most compelling story about their unlucky confrontation with the highwayman.

When he returned with large glasses of lemonade for Velina and Johnny, there was also a plate of biscuits and slices of cake.

"That's scrumptious!" Johnny exclaimed. "I didn't have time to finish up all my luncheon."

"You must forget about it," the Marquis answered, "and no one is to be told about the highwayman."

"It was very frightening," Johnny murmured. "He wanted Samson, but he might have taken Hunter as well."

"He might have done that or, if he had gone away with Samson and Fireball, we would have been left with his dilapidated-looking nag to carry us all and perhaps you would have had to run along behind with Jimmie!"

Johnny laughed.

"I did not think the 'ighwayman's 'orse was a good one," Johnny said, "but what will 'appen to 'im now?"

"I expect some kind farmer will pick him up and see that he is comfortable and well-fed and he will soon forget that he has ever had to carry a wicked man like the highwayman."

"Now drink up your lemonade," Velina prompted.

"Yes, we must move on," the Marquis said. "Even if we are tired, I want to be many miles away from what was left of the highwayman before we stop for the night."

It was an issue that Velina did not want to argue about, but she did realise that Johnny was exhausted.

When he was mounted, she told him to start riding towards the entrance of the yard.

She was holding Samson when the Marquis joined her and in a whisper she said to him,

"Johnny is becoming tired and you are right for us to be safe after all, but he is only a little boy."

"And you are a very beautiful and brave girl," the Marquis murmured.

There was a note in his voice and a look in his eye that made her feel shy.

When he lifted her onto Fireball, she said,

"You must do what you think is best, Neil, and I don't want to argue with you about it."

"You can say anything you like," he replied. "And I have a great deal to say to you when we are alone."

He turned away as he spoke and mounted Samson.

Then they were away, but now the Marquis rode slower.

About six-thirty they came to quite a pleasant little village and it had a better built and larger inn than they had encountered before.

They trotted into the yard as they always did and found for the first time that there was an ostler to help them with their horses.

"I had better see if there is a room here for us to stay the night," the Marquis said to the man.

"There be plenty of empty beds," the ostler replied. "We've 'ad a bad season and things ain't goin' as well as they ought to be."

The Marquis left Samson with him and walked into the inn.

There was no doubt that the publican was delighted to accommodate them.

When he ordered dinner and said that he wanted it to be a specially appetising one, the cook, who he gathered was not the publican's wife, was then full of suggestions as to what they might enjoy.

In fact it was after such an excellent meal that the publican blurted out apologetically,

"I'm sure you'll understand, sir, if I asks you to pay somethin' in advance. Things have been bad up here this past year and a number of visitors having spent the night found their pockets were empty in the mornin'."

"I can understand your difficulties," the Marquis agreed, "and, of course, you are being sensible."

He put several gold sovereigns down on the table and added,

"If the bill tomorrow morning comes to more than this, I will, of course, settle it. I assure you that I have the cash to do so."

It was not surprising when they came in after seeing that the horses were comfortable, that they were taken to what the Marquis was sure were their best rooms.

There were two large rooms for Velina and himself facing the front of the inn, with a smaller one on the other side of the passage for Johnny and the publican made no fuss about him having Jimmie with him.

Velina was afraid that they might, as this inn was obviously greatly superior to the places they had stayed in previously.

She was delighted to find that there was a bathroom on the same floor as their bedrooms and she was sure that it was the only one in the inn.

When Velina tried to see if the hot water worked, it actually came out of the tap.

"Johnny must have a bath first," she suggested.

As Johnny ran along the passage to have a look at it, she said to the Marquis,

"I see that there is a shop across the street. Do you think you could be very kind and buy Johnny a clean shirt which he badly needs and also a jumper. I can give you the money now or when you come back."

"I should have thought of it myself," the Marquis replied. "But we have not seen a shop that would have sold that sort of item, have we?"

"We did not look for one and I expect we would have found one if we had, but I kept quiet about it."

He smiled at her.

"You are a remarkable girl. But I understand that, when we arrive at your aunt's, we must try to look our best. Otherwise she may well refuse to have such down-at-heel travellers in her house!"

Velina grinned, but she did not contradict him.

He went off to the shop taking with him Johnny's shirt. Although it had been washed, it was still stained in some places and was definitely torn in others.

The Marquis came back with two shirts that might have been bought in a shop in London.

There was also a very nice red woollen jumper that was very different from the ragged one he was wearing that had grown worse every time he took it off or put it on.

"You are clever to have found these," Velina said. "I know that Johnny will be thrilled with them."

"If you are going to worry now about my clothes," the Marquis replied, "I assure you that I have a clean shirt in my bag and so I hope you will not be ashamed of me."

"I am not likely to be," Velina answered, "when you have been so kind."

She had carried up from the yard the bags that hung from Fireball's saddle and they were standing just inside the bedroom that Velina was to use.

The Marquis looked at her intently and then said,

"I have a feeling that if we have a chance we should all go shopping before we see your aunt."

"What you are saying politely," Velina replied, "is that we look almost like tramps. It's not surprising since we have ridden so far and there have been such terrible things happening to us."

The Marquis did not answer and walked away to his own room.

Velina made her hair as tidy as she could, hoping that when she went downstairs to dinner he would not be ashamed of her.

Actually there was no one in the dining room to see them.

Johnny, after his bath, was so pleased with his clean shirt and new jumper that he did not appear to be as tired as Velina expected him to be.

However, he had his meal first before theirs was ready and Velina then took him upstairs to put him to bed.

"I want to stay up and see what you are eating," Johnny grumbled.

"You must be strong and fit enough to ride Hunter tomorrow," Velina told him. "If you don't have your sleep tonight, you might go to sleep when you are riding him and fall to the ground, then he could go on without you."

"Hunter would wait for me," Johnny told her. "He loves me as I love 'im."

"Of course he does, but you must not make Jimmie jealous."

"I love Jimmie and I love you," Johnny said.

"And I love you," Velina answered. "Now you go to sleep and tomorrow you may be staying in a very big house, much bigger than this."

"I'll like that and Jimmie'll like it too."

"He has been a very good dog coming all this long way with us," Velina replied.

She patted Jimmie as she spoke.

Then she bent and kissed Johnny.

"Now say your prayers," she insisted. "I am sure you have not forgotten the one we said together last night."

"No, I remember every word, but I think we should say a prayer for the poor 'ighwayman. If 'e's dead 'e'll go to Hell, won't 'e?"

"He's not dead!" Velina assured him. "So that need not worry you. He will have a very sore arm and perhaps after that he will stop being a highwayman."

"I wonder what 'e'll do?" Johnny asked. "It must be difficult for an 'ighwayman to get a job 'cos people'll be scared of 'im."

"I don't suppose he will say he is a highwayman," Velina told him. "As you know, you have been told not to talk about him, so you must not mention him again. Just forget he ever existed."

"I can't do that, miss. I keep thinkin' about 'im and 'ow 'e fell off 'is 'orse."

"Well, you heard what Mr. Neil said about him. He said we were not to mention him in case people made us talk about what happened," Velina reminded him.

"I'll only talk about 'im to you," Johnny replied.

She kissed him again, saying,

"Now I am going downstairs for dinner. If you are frightened in the night or want anything, you know I am in the room just opposite you."

Johnny nodded and she kissed him again.

"You have been wonderful on this long journey," she told him, "but I don't want you to be too tired before we arrive at the big house."

She pulled the curtains across so that the room was in darkness.

Then she went out of the door and she was aware as she did so that Johnny was almost asleep and that Jimmie had jumped up onto the bed to lie at the end of it.

She thought wistfully to herself that she would miss them both when their odyssey was over.

Then she went down the stairs to find the Marquis waiting impatiently for her because the first course of their dinner had already arrived.

"As it is our last night on the road," he said, "I have ordered champagne."

Velina's eyes widened.

"Are you quite sure that you can afford it, Neil?" she asked.

"I think it important for us to have something with which to drink our health. Also to congratulate ourselves on having achieved what I think anyone would describe as an unusual and intriguing journey."

"It is certainly something I did not expect," Velina replied. "I am sure that if we told people about it no one would believe that we could find such a delightful little boy as Johnny in such a strange way."

There was silence between them for a moment.

Then the Marquis said,

"You are not to worry about him, although I know you are. I am sure that I will find a couple who can look after him and treat him as if he was their own."

"I was thinking the same," she added. "Of course we will have to decide who can make the best offer."

The Marquis laughed.

"That is true, but I suppose being a woman you are sure to think that your choice is better than mine."

"I think everything you have arranged so far has been absolutely splendid," Velina said. "When I say my prayers, I thank God every night that I was brave enough to ask if I could ride beside you."

"Well, we have most certainly had an adventure," the Marquis smiled.

He thought as he spoke that was what he had set out to find from the very beginning.

And it had certainly come true.

In fact there would be no argument about whether or not he had won his bet with the Duke.

"You are looking so serious, Neil" Velina observed. "What is worrying you?"

"Actually it is what has been worrying me for some time," the Marquis replied. "It is what I am to do about you."

"About – me?" Velina asked.

"Well, it appears to me, although I might be wrong, that your stepfather, if he really does want you to marry this man he has chosen, will undoubtedly not give up his search for you. Even though the first effort failed."

Velina shivered.

"I have thought of that, too," she said. "But I am sure that my aunt will stand up for me and tell him that he has no right to force me into matrimony with anyone."

"Is your aunt married?" the Marquis asked.

Velina shook her head.

"No, she is a widow. She is my father's sister, not my mother's."

"Do you really think that she will be able to control or better still refute your stepfather's wishes?" the Marquis quizzed.

Velina was quiet for a moment.

Then she said,

"Please will you come with me to meet my aunt? I think that you are intending to leave me at the door, but you are so clever and so wise I feel that you will save me if she insists that I go back to my stepfather."

"Why should she do that?" the Marquis asked.

Velina shrugged her shoulders.

"She is rather impressed by him and then she might think that he knows better than she does what is good for me."

"It could not be good for any woman to marry a man she does not love," the Marquis replied.

He was thinking that so many women did so, either because the man in question, like himself, boasted a title or because he was rich.

"You may think – it very silly of me," Velina said in a hesitating voice, "but I always thought that one day I would find someone I loved who would love me. Then we would be married – because what we have for each other is the real love that people write about in books."

"Which sometimes really does happen in real life," the Marquis added.

"Do you sincerely believe that?" Velina asked. "It is what I want to believe, but I have been so frightened in case it will never happen."

There was silence for a moment and then he said,

"We know very little about each other. In fact, I do not know your real name any more than you know mine. But suppose I said I was in love with you."

Velina's eyes widened.

Then, as she looked at him, she looked away shyly.

"I am waiting for your answer," the Marquis said.

"I think you would only say something like that if it was true," Velina replied.

"You are quite right. I would never say anything important to you that was not true."

Before she could say anything more, the publican, who had been waiting on them, brought in the coffee and a liqueur that he thought the Marquis would like.

"Both of us have enjoyed our dinner enormously," the Marquis told him, "and thank you for all the trouble you have taken over it."

"It's been a real pleasure to cook things that most of the people round here don't even know the name of," the publican replied.

"Then why do you stay here?" the Marquis asked.

He had known while he was eating the meal that it would certainly not have appealed to the average traveller even if they had heard of it.

But the majority of people travelling North would take the main road and not wander, as they had done, round the lanes where there were small villages.

"It be a long story, sir. I had the chance of takin' over this inn from a man who owed me money and it was that or nothin', so I took the inn."

"Of course you did," the Marquis approved, "and it is very charming and very comfortable. In fact, I will tell people about it when I return to London. I feel sure that you will have a lot more visitors one way or another."

The publican flushed with excitement.

"That be real kind of you, sir," he said, "and I can see you're a gentleman who'll keep your word."

"You must not expect them to come immediately," the Marquis answered, "but, as there are a great number of people going North, especially if there is racing or shooting in the autumn, I will certainly tell my friends to stay here with you."

The man was clearly overcome with the Marquis's kindness and, when he withdrew, Velina commented,

"It was wonderful of you, Neil, to tell him that. He has tried to please us in every possible way."

"If nothing else he is an excellent cook and that is what pleases most people when they are travelling."

"Yes, of course it is," Velina agreed. "I am sure if he has even a few guests every month, he will be able to keep his head above water."

"I will make sure that he does," the Marquis said. "I know a lot of people who come North in the autumn for the grouse shooting and the salmon fishing."

"Because my father has been dead since I was very young," Velina told him, "I had forgotten that was the fashionable way of enjoying the autumn."

"Well, now I think that you should go to bed," the Marquis said, "because I agree it has been a very tiring day and I am certain that young Johnny is fast asleep by now."

"He was almost asleep before I left him and so was Jimmie who, of course, was sleeping on his bed."

"Then I am certain that neither of them will worry you in the night," the Marquis said, "and nor will I."

He thought as he spoke that many of the women he knew would think that an insult.

But Velina merely replied,

"I expect that you will fall asleep as soon as your head touches the pillow, as I know I will."

They walked up the stairs together.

Velina peeped into Johnny's room and saw, as she expected, that he was fast asleep.

She shut the door very quietly and then he said,

"Now you have nothing to worry about."

He opened the door of her bedroom for her to go in.

She stopped in the doorway.

"Goodnight, Neil," she whispered, "and thank you for being so kind."

"And I want to thank you most sincerely, Velina, for saving my horse and perhaps my life."

He spoke very quietly.

Then he put his arms round her and pulled her close to him.

"There is only one way I can really thank you," he murmured.

Then his lips were on hers.

It had given her a strange sensation when his lips had touched hers earlier that day.

But at this moment when he was kissing her gently but determinedly and his arms were round her, it was the most exciting and thrilling thing that had ever happened.

She only knew that it was as if her heart turned a somersault.

At the same time the Marquis was carrying her up into the sky.

Then, when she felt that it was impossible to feel more than she was feeling already, the Marquis raised his head.

In a voice that did not sound like his own he said,

"I love you, Velina, and I want to know if you love me?"

"I love you, I love you," Velina whispered. "I did not know that love was so marvellous and sublime."

The Marquis kissed her again.

Then, almost before she could be aware of it, she was inside her bedroom, the door was closed and she was alone.

CHAPTER SEVEN

The sun was streaming through the window when Velina woke.

As she did so, she felt a sudden brilliant happiness, almost as if the sunshine was inside her.

She had taken a long time to fall sleep because she was thinking of Neil and how wonderful he was.

'He is so kind and understanding and he is so much a man,' she thought.

She had never met anyone like him and she just knew instinctively that he was everything a man should be.

No one else would have behaved so kindly to her and prevented her from being frightened on such a long and arduous ride.

The door opened a little and then Johnny peeped into the room.

"Can I get up, please, miss?" he asked.

"Yes, of course," she answered. "Don't forget to wash yourself and you have to look very smart today."

"Why?" he questioned.

"Because we are coming to the end of our journey and there will be people who will want to meet you."

Johnny stood hesitatingly for a moment.

Then he asked,

"Suppose they don't like me and send me back to my uncle?"

"No one will do that," Velina insisted firmly. "You know that Mr. Neil has said that he will find you a home if I cannot find you one myself."

Johnny stood looking at her for a moment.

Then he said rather hesitantly,

"I – want to stay – with you."

"And I want you to stay with me, but it may not be possible. Anyway we need not talk about it now. Hurry up, Johnny, as I expect there will be a delicious breakfast downstairs."

Johnny went away.

Velina wished she had not put into his mind that he would have to leave her.

'But I am not certain yet where I will go myself,' she thought.

She knew, however, just where she wanted to go.

But suppose by this morning that Neil had changed his mind and did not want her after all.

'I love him so much!' she thought. 'I would scrub the floor and keep the smallest cottage nice for him if he cannot afford anything better.'

Then she was thinking that Samson must be a very valuable stallion.

Yet, if that was all he possessed, he would have to find some way of making money for both of them, if they were to be married.

Then she told herself that nothing mattered except that he loved her and she loved him.

'This is exactly what I have always wanted,' she told herself, 'and why I ran away.'

She said a prayer of thankfulness to God that she had found anyone as wonderful as Neil.

Then she began to dress herself quickly because she was going to him again.

He was downstairs in the dining room and Johnny was with him when she joined them.

The Marquis rose from the table and greeted her,

"Good morning, Velina. You look like spring itself and no woman could be more entrancing."

Velina gave a little laugh.

"Now you are spoiling me with flattery and I am enjoying every word."

Colour had come to her cheeks and she was smiling as she sat down beside the Marquis.

"Did you sleep well?" he asked.

"Of course I did," she replied.

"I hope you dreamt of me."

She did not answer him because her breakfast was brought in at that moment and placed in front of her.

It was a far better breakfast than anything they had had on their journey so far.

As she finished up with toast and marmalade, she hoped that the bill was not too much for Neil to pay.

Johnny, who had finished, ran from the room to see if the horses were all right.

Velina turned to Neil and said,

"Please let me pay for what was spent last night and now. I am afraid it will be much larger than anything you have had to pay before. I think that we have been rather extravagant."

The Marquis smiled.

"Most women would expect a man to pay for them whether he could afford it or not."

"Not if they love him," she said without thinking.

Then, as she realised that she had used the word 'love', which was something he had not said this morning, she blushed.

He thought that nothing could be more attractive than the flush against her white skin and the shyness in her blue eyes.

"I love you! I do love you," he said very quietly. "And I will never allow any other man to pay for anything you require."

"I am only thinking of you," Velina replied quietly.

"It is something that I find very unusual," he said, "and it makes me love you more than I do already."

Because she had no words to answer him, Velina blushed again.

Then she murmured,

"We still have quite a long way to go and I think we should leave as soon as you are ready."

"I will go and pay the bill," the Marquis told her.

As he went off to do so, Velina hurried up to her room to collect her bag and hat and then she looked into Johnny's room to make sure he had left nothing behind.

There was only his old shirt and jumper that she had thrown into the waste-paper basket last night and he thought that he would certainly make a good impression on her aunt.

Perhaps if she was staying with her, he would be allowed to stay too.

Then she thought of Neil and wondered if he would want to marry her at once or perhaps wait until they went South again.

It seemed extraordinary that having been with him so long, she had no idea where his home was and whether his parents were still living and if he had any brothers and sisters.

It was almost as if they had made a pact with each other not to talk about themselves. But he had not asked her questions just as she had not asked him any.

However, there was still Samson to say that he was certainly not completely penniless.

Unless he had won the stallion as a bet in some way or other, he must have cost him a large sum of money even if he had bought him when he was merely a foal.

All these thoughts passed through her mind.

At the same time her heart was still singing because Neil loved her.

To be near him made her feel head-over-heels in love with him.

When she walked down the stairs, Neil and Johnny were bringing the horses from the stables.

They had saddled and bridled them and Velina saw that they would need a really good brush-down when they reached her aunt's stables.

When the publican came to say goodbye to them, Velina thanked him profusely for his delicious food and very comfortable bed.

"I hope you'll come again," he said.

"Whenever we are going South, of course we will," Velina replied.

"You can be sure of that," the Marquis added. "As I promised you, I will tell my friends how comfortable we have been and how excellent your food is."

The publican was delighted.

As they rode off, Velina said,

"You have made him very happy. I hope you have enough friends coming North to show that you have kept your promise."

"I think really you are questioning whether I have friends who shoot grouse in the autumn and enjoy fishing for salmon," the Marquis replied.

"Yes, that is true," Velina agreed a little shyly.

"One of the many things I really adore about you," the Marquis said, "is that you tell the truth. There are far too many people in the world today who lie because it suits them or else they are afraid of facing up to something that they find distasteful."

"I try never to lie," Velina replied, "and I don't think that I have ever lied to you."

"I would know if you had," he retorted. "There is such an expression of honesty and purity in your eyes that if they changed I should immediately be aware of it."

Velina held up her hands.

"Now you are frightening me," she exclaimed.

"I am merely telling you the truth, Velina, and I do agree that it is something which frightens quite a number of people."

Velina laughed at his remark.

He lifted her up to put her on Fireball's back.

For a moment he held her close to him instead of setting her down on the saddle.

"I love you," he said very quietly.

There was no need for her to tell him that she loved him. The expression on her face said it without words.

Just for a moment he gazed at her before he set her down on the saddle and she picked up the reins.

He lifted Johnny, who was playing with Jimmie, on to Hunter and then he mounted Samson.

"I think it is safe to let Jimmie run behind us," he said to Johnny. "But if he tires he can ride with me."

"It's good for him to use his legs," Johnny replied. "But he was very tired last night."

"I think we all were. Now don't go too fast through the village, but we will quicken our pace when we are clear of the cottages."

Velina was already ahead, having waved goodbye to the cook who was standing at the kitchen window.

As the Marquis joined her, she sighed,

"We have been so lucky with the weather. It might have rained every day and then we should have had to wait as none of us appear to have a raincoat with us."

"Well, you and Johnny left in a hurry," the Marquis said, "but actually it is something I did not think of myself, although I should have."

Velina longed to ask him where he had come from and where his home was.

But they had both been so very careful not to ask uncomfortable questions ever since they met that she felt it would be a mistake to appear curious until he was ready to tell her about himself.

They found a road that was not fenced in on either side and galloped the horses freely on the grass.

When it was getting near to luncheon time, Velina knew that the Marquis was looking out for an inn where they could eat and the horses could rest.

It was not as easy as it had been yesterday, but finally they reached a pretty little village where there was a tea-shop.

The Marquis told Velina to wait and hold his horse while he went inside to see if they could provide them with anything substantial.

But Velina felt that if he used his charm as he had done everywhere they been so far, he would undoubtedly get his own way.

She was quite right.

When he returned a few minutes later, he said that they could provide fresh eggs and sausages if they thought that was a large enough luncheon for them.

"Of course it is," Velina said, "how clever of you to persuade them to have us."

"It's clean and cosy and who could ask for more."

They sat down in the garden under an umbrella.

No one enjoyed their luncheon more than Johnny and Jimmie, who had a piece of sausage from everyone.

Now they set off again.

Velina knew that they were only a mile or so from her aunt's house.

Despite herself, she still felt reluctant to go there, in case there was any difficulty about Neil or Johnny.

If she admitted that she and Neil were in love, her aunt would obviously want to know who he was and where he came from.

She felt it would be uncomfortable to admit that she could answer no questions about him, except that she loved him.

Now the countryside was very beautiful and Velina felt that it was a fitting background for their love.

It would be marvellous to be alone with him where no one could interfere or ask awkward questions.

Then she knew it was all part of her fear of what lay ahead.

Perhaps her aunt would say that she must obey her stepfather and return home and she could feel the fear of everything that had happened creeping over her.

Quite unexpectedly the Marquis quizzed her,

"What is worrying you, Velina?"

"How do you know I am worried?"

"I know what you are thinking and feeling just as you know the same about me," he answered. "The truth is, darling, we belong to each other already and I know now that I have been looking for you all my life and perhaps in another life when I was unable to find you."

"The other half of each other," Velina murmured. "That is what the Ancient Greeks believe we seek and what I always hoped and prayed I would find."

"And you have found it now," the Marquis replied, "just as I have."

She looked up at him.

He knew the answer without her saying it in words.

"Don't be frightened, my precious darling," he said, "everything will be all right and our journey at its end will be the beginning of yet another and even more marvellous one."

It was impossible for Velina not to believe him.

She was smiling as a little while later they turned in through some very imposing-looking gates and started to ride up a long drive.

The Marquis was carrying Jimmie on the front of his saddle and Johnny was trotting ahead on Hunter.

Suddenly they saw straight in front of them a large and most attractive house and Johnny turned his head back to say,

"Is this where we are staying? It's big, as big as a Palace."

Velina turned her head towards the Marquis.

"We have arrived," she said, "and I only hope that my aunt is here and will not be too surprised to see me."

"You are not to worry," the Marquis answered. "I will make everything as clear as I can and all you have to do is to trust me."

"You know I do, Neil," Velina replied.

At the same time she wanted to be in his arms.

But Johnny had quickened his pace and reached the courtyard before they did.

"It's the biggest 'ouse I've ever seen," he enthused. "Are we really going to stay 'ere?"

"I hope so," Velina answered.

As she was speaking, two grooms appeared to take their horses.

When they asked no questions, she felt as if they were already expecting them.

The Marquis dismounted and then gave Jimmie to Johnny.

"Hold him in your arms," he said. "People don't like strange dogs roaming about in their house."

"I'll 'old 'im," Johnny agreed obediently.

They walked up the steps to the front door, which opened as they reached it.

Velina saw waiting for them was the butler who had been there ever since she could remember.

"Good afternoon, Batley," she said.

The butler smiled at her.

"It's nice to see you, my Lady," he replied. "Her Ladyship's waiting for you in the drawing room. She said that I were to bring you to her as soon as you arrived."

Bewildered, Velina looked at the Marquis.

He handed his hat to one of the footmen.

Then, as the butler began to walk ahead of them, Velina slipped her hand into the Marquis's.

"I am so frightened," she whispered.

"You are not to be!" he answered.

They walked down the passage that was decorated with fine pictures and some inlaid furniture.

Then he opened the door of what Velina knew was the drawing room and announced loudly,

"Lady Velina's just arrived, my Lady."

Velina walked in.

Then she stood still.

It was impossible for her to move.

Standing beside her aunt in front of the mantelpicce was *her stepfather.*

"Oh, here you are, Velina," her aunt began. "I have been so worried. I thought you would have arrived sooner. I see that you have brought some friends with you."

"I, too, was wondering what had happened to you, Velina," her stepfather blurted out in a harsh voice.

He was a most unpleasant-looking man and Velina thought that he looked even more frightening than he had when she had ran away.

Velina's aunt moved forward, kissed her and said,

"Now introduce me to your friends."

"There is no need to do that!" her stepfather said sharply. "If she has met friends on the road, that is where they belong and where they can return. Velina is coming back immediately with me to London where she will marry Sir Stephen Harbut as I have arranged."

Velina gave a cry of horror and reached out towards the Marquis.

His hands closed over hers and he realised that she was trembling.

"I am afraid," he said, "that what you have arranged must now be cancelled."

"And who the devil are you to give me orders?" Velina's stepfather asked angrily. "If you picked her up on the road, as you have no right to do, you can take yourself and that child, who I suppose is yours, back on the road again. As this young lady's stepfather, I am her Guardian by law until she is twenty-one."

Velina's fingers quivered in the Marquis's hands.

He could tell how frightened she was.

"As you are being so offensive," the Marquis said coolly, "it would be correct for me to tell you that Velina has promised to be my wife and so we are engaged to be married."

"Engaged!" Velina's aunt exclaimed. "Oh my dear, are you wise to marry in such a hurry?"

"She is going to be married in a hurry, but not to this stranger," her stepfather shouted out angrily. "He is obviously after her money and I am not fool enough to let him have it."

"That happens to be entirely untrue," the Marquis said quietly. "In fact, although I can hardly expect you to believe it, Velina has promised to become my wife without knowing who I am and I do not even know her name."

"You can hardly expect me to be taken in by that lie," her stepfather sneered. "You know perfectly well that, as her father and mother are dead, she inherits her father's estate and is therefore a rich heiress. It was a good effort on your part to make her agree to marry you. But I assure you that it will be over my dead body. So the sooner you get out of here, the better it will be for you!"

The Marquis turned quite calmly towards Velina's aunt.

"I can only beg you to excuse this offensive scene in your drawing room. I think I must introduce myself and I am, as it happens, the Marquis of Whisinford."

For a moment there was complete silence.

Not only did Velina's aunt and stepfather stare at him, but also at Velina.

It was Johnny who broke the silence by running to the Marquis's side.

"If they send you away," he said, "please – can I come with you?"

"They are not going to send me away," the Marquis replied. "I can only apologise, Velina, that this unseemly behaviour on behalf of your stepfather should upset you."

She looked at him and whispered,

"I had no idea who you are."

"I thought you were far too beautiful to be anything but an angel just dropped down from Heaven," the Marquis answered.

He spoke in a quiet voice, but it was impossible for Velina's aunt and stepfather not to hear what he said.

Then her aunt moved towards him.

"If you are really the Marquis of Whisinford," she said, "my brother knew your father. He used to shoot with him at your lovely house in Oxfordshire."

"You will think it rather strange," he replied, "but Velina and I, although we fell in love, did not tell each other who we were. Therefore I should be very grateful if you would tell me the name of your brother and, of course, yourself."

"My brother was the Duke of Belverton and I am Lady Cecily Belvedere."

"Then I think you must have stayed at Whisinford Park with your brother!" the Marquis exclaimed. "I thought that I recognised you when I came into the room."

"And I do remember you," Lady Cecily said. "You were a dear little boy and not much older than this boy who must be one of your relatives."

"On the contrary. Velina and I met him on the road and, as he is an orphan, we are hoping very much to find a home for him."

"I don't believe any of all this," Velina's stepfather snarled angrily.

"Well, it happens to be true," the Marquis replied. "I therefore suggest that, as this is a family meeting, you have the decency to withdraw. Let us discuss our personal affairs without any interruption or aggression."

Before there could be a reply, Lady Cecily put her hand on Velina's stepfather's arm and suggested,

"The Marquis is right. I think it would be wise if you moved into another room. It is now obvious that your journey is quite unnecessary and you should return home."

She spoke so sensibly and quietly that it was with difficulty that the Marquis did not applaud her.

She made it impossible for the disagreeable man to reply or to do anything at all but leave them alone.

Without saying a word he marched out of the room slamming the door noisily behind him.

Velina gave a little cry.

"Oh! That was so splendid of you, Aunt Cecily. I have been so terrified that he would forbid me to marry Neil, but I had no idea that – he is a Marquis."

"Does it matter?" the Marquis asked.

"Not in the slightest," Velina replied with a smile.

Just for a moment the Marquis wanted to close his eyes at the wonder of it all.

He had always wanted to be loved for himself and not for his title and it was exactly what had now happened.

He knew that Velina would have married him if he had really been Neil Barlow.

And he realised that she was right in thinking that they had found the other half of each other.

Lady Cecily was drawing Velina away from the Marquis towards the sofa.

"Come and sit down and tell me all about it," she suggested. "Why did you two not know who you were?"

"We met on the road as I was running away from my horrible stepfather," Velina answered. "He wanted me to marry a man I knew was only interested in the money that Mama left me."

"So you did run away," Lady Cecily said. "I think that was very brave of you."

"I might have been very frightened if Neil had not been riding alone and I asked if I could ride beside him."

"What about the little boy?" Lady Cecily asked.

As he was bored with the conversation, Johnny had sat down on the floor and was playing a game with Jimmie.

Velina told her how they had found Johnny being beaten by his cruel uncle and how they had tried to find his mother.

"She was dead," Velina whispered, "but we have not told Johnny yet. Because he has been so happy with us I don't think that he really misses her."

"You say they lived in a cottage?"

"Well, his mother's father was the Verger in the local Church," Velina said, "but I think that his father was just a labourer."

"So he is an orphan?"

Velina nodded.

"I am certain I can find him a family at The Hall, who will be only too pleased to take him in," the Marquis broke in to say.

"I know of a family too," Lady Cecily added.

"Not Batley!" Velina exclaimed.

"You might remember that Batley's wife is younger than him and her only son, who was born six years ago died from appendicitis three months ago. She is broken-hearted and I doubt if she is young enough to have another child."

"I have known Batley ever since I was a little girl," Velina said. "He is a very nice man and I love Mrs. Batley too."

"Then we will talk about it later," Lady Cecily said. "But now I hope that awful stepfather of yours is leaving. I thought when he told me you had run away from the man he wanted you to marry, that it was a very sensible thing for you to do. But, of course, I did not expect you to find anyone so charming as Neil who I knew when he was a little boy."

Then she smiled at the Marquis who sighed,

"I had not the faintest idea that Velina was your brother's daughter."

"I am sure that she will be very happy at The Hall," Lady Cecily replied. "It is the most gorgeous house I have ever visited. And Velina will make you a beautiful wife."

"That is exactly what I thought myself. I think you will understand, Lady Cecily, when I tell you that I wanted to be loved for myself and not for my possessions."

"And you met on the road – the road to romance," Lady Cecily cried. "It's the most heavenly story I ever heard and should be put into a book."

"It is unbelievably romantic for me," Velina said, gazing at the Marquis.

"Now what you need to do is to have a bath and change for dinner," Lady Cecily said. "I shall be so glad if that ghastly stepfather of yours has departed. Then we will be alone and we can plan your wedding."

"That is exactly what I intend to do," the Marquis replied. "But I would welcome the evening more if I could be properly dressed."

Lady Cecily smiled.

"I think you will find a surprise for you upstairs."

The Marquis looked at her questioningly.

"A surprise?" he enquired.

"You had better come and look for yourself," Lady Cecily answered. "As I am sure you are tired after riding such a long way, we will have dinner early so that you can make up for the sleep you have missed on your very long journey."

"It has been a long, but a very exciting one," Velina said, "and we will tell you all about it later."

"Well, now I am going to take you up to your rooms," Lady Cecily replied. "Batley will take this little boy to his wife and I am sure that she would like to look after him."

Mrs. Batley was the cook and Velina remembered her as a very friendly woman. When she was small and had stayed with her aunt, Mrs. Batley had always cooked special dishes for her and sent her favourite cakes up to the nursery.

They walked from the room and along the passage.

As they did so, they saw a carriage moving away from the front door.

It contained Velina's stepfather.

She was so thrilled to see him departing that she slipped her arm into the Marquis's.

"He has gone back to London!" she cried.

"I thought he would," the Marquis replied. "Forget him! You need never see him again."

"If that is not true, at least he will not interfere," Lady Cecily said. "I always thought him a snob when he was married to your mother. I am quite certain now as you are to marry Neil that he will be trying to ingratiate himself with you rather than fighting against your marriage."

"I am so glad, so very glad about that," Velina said.

The Marquis smiled down at her.

"I am still prepared to run away with you if it is necessary!" he told her.

Velina then pressed her cheek onto his arm and he thought it was a very touching gesture.

Batley moved from the front door, which had been closed by one of the footmen.

Lady Cecily went up to him.

"I want you, Batley, to take this boy to your wife. He has ridden a very long way with Lady Velina and his Lordship and I am sure he must be thirsty and tired."

"My wife'd love to look after him," Batley said.

He put out his hand and took hold of Johnny's.

"Come along and let's see what we can find for you and that nice dog to eat. I expects he's hungry too."

"We 'ad a good luncheon," Johnny told him, "but we 'ad no tea and Jimmie's always 'ungry at this hour."

"And you are too," Batley said. "Now come along, young man."

They disappeared down the passage that led to the kitchen and Velina and the Marquis followed Lady Cecily up the stairs.

"As I told you," Lady Cecily said to the Marquis, "there is a surprise for you in this room."

She opened the door.

To his astonishment the Marquis saw Herbert, his trusty valet, standing by the dressing table.

"Herbert!" he exclaimed. "How on earth did you get here?"

Herbert laughed.

"I thought your Lordship'd be surprised. I drove up rather than goin' by sea as you had suggested. At the first hotel I stayed at I found Lady Velina's stepfather who said his stepdaughter had run away from him. His valet and I became friendly and he tells me that the young lady was bein' forced by her stepfather into matrimony to a man who was after her money."

Velina was listening wide-eyed at what was being said, as Herbert continued,

"His valet and I arranged to meet at the next place, which was on the main road. It was there the three men turned up to say they'd seen her Ladyship on Fireball, but you'd escaped during the night."

The Marquis laughed.

"It was very clever the way we did that."

"So I gathers, my Lord," Herbert said. "But her Ladyship's stepfather went into a terrible rage and said that they wouldn't have a penny from him unless they found you again. It was then I learns that he thought her Ladyship was goin' to her aunt in Yorkshire. He said the man who was with her was ridin' a horse called Samson."

Again the Marquis laughed.

"So that is how you found out where I was."

"I didn't have to put two and two together to guess that," Herbert replied, "so I comes here. But, of course, I didn't tell them who you was, my Lord, as you'd told me you was travellin' in disguise for a bet."

"I have not had time to tell you everything, but you shall hear it all tonight. All I can say is that I am delighted to see you, Herbert, and I will have a change of clothes. I am sick to death of being Mr. Barlow in this outfit!"

"I'm not surprised, my Lord."

As he had his bath, the Marquis was wondering whether his adventures, which certainly were fantastic and would please the Duke, would be topped by those that Lord Alfred would encounter on his journey to Land's End.

'At least we will have something to talk about,' he said to himself, 'when we next meet at White's.'

Then he found it difficult to think of anything but Velina.

She and Lady Cecily left the Marquis talking to his valet and crossed the corridor to where there was a lovely room with a four-poster bed.

A maid was unpacking the things that Fireball had carried for her.

"It's not fair," Velina said. "Neil has all his best clothes with him, but I only have one dress that I am tired of wearing."

"I am sure we can find you something, my dearest child," her aunt said. "Your cousin, Arabella, often stays here and last time she told me that she had left many of her clothes behind when she went to Edinburgh."

"Oh, please Aunt Cecily, find one pretty dress for me so that I will look attractive for Neil."

"I will," Lady Cecily said. "So come now and look in the room Arabella always has when she stays here."

They found the room further down the passage and, at the wardrobe, Velina gave a cry of delight.

Her cousin, Arabella, was just the same size as she was and she had left a large selection of evening gowns.

"I am sure they will fit you and anything that is too big can be pinned to make it smaller," her aunt advised.

Velina kissed her and went on,

"Thank you, thank you, for being so kind to me. I was so frightened that you would be shocked by Neil and send him away."

"My dearest, I am simply thrilled that you are to marry anyone so delightful. His father and yours were the greatest of friends. Although unfortunately your father died early in the War you must be aware of how popular he was with all the people who really mattered and that, of course, included the Marquis of Whisinford."

Velina kissed her aunt again.

Then she went to her bedroom for a scented bath and to be helped into the evening dress that belonged to her cousin. It was a very soft pink trimmed with real lace and embroidered with diamanté on the bodice.

Then when she went down the stairs, she felt that at last the Marquis would see her the way she wanted to look.

Batley was in the hall and Velina said to him,

"I feel that I have rather neglected Johnny. Is he all right with you?"

"Come and see him, my Lady," Batley suggested.

He took her down the passage to the kitchen and, as he opened the door, Velina heard Johnny laughing.

They went in and he was sitting at the kitchen table eating what appeared to be something really delicious from the plate in front of him.

However, when he saw her, he then jumped down and ran towards her saying,

"I've somethin' special to show you! Something you'll think very lovely, miss."

Velina took his hand in hers as he pulled her across the kitchen.

In the far corner, she saw a collie dog sitting in a large basket and beside the dog were two small puppies.

"They were born two days ago," Johnny was saying excitedly. "I've been tryin' to think of names for them."

"I am sure you can think of very good ones," Velina answered. "But what does Jimmie think about it?"

"He likes them very much as I do and I'm goin' to play with them when they're bigger."

Velina looked up at Batley and smiled.

"He loves all animals," she told him, "and he has ridden a long way. In fact he is a very sporting little boy."

"That's what I thought," Batley replied.

Velina moved to one side so that she could speak to Batley without Johnny hearing.

"He is an orphan," she told him. "Both his father and mother are dead and his only relation is a cruel wicked man."

"I know what you're saying alright, my Lady. It'll be a miracle for the Missus to look after him. She's been ever so miserable ever since our little 'un passed over and already she's smiling as I've not seen her smile for weeks."

"I cannot imagine two people more suitable to look after Johnny than you and Mrs. Batley," Velina murmured.

She thought as she spoke that tomorrow she would give Batley some money to spend on clothes for Johnny and would make him understand that she was responsible for any expenses that he and his wife may incur.

"I thinks," he was saying, "the little boy'd be happy if he slept down here next to us. I've told him he can have the room that opens into the garden so that his dog can run out whenever he wants to."

"That will be wonderful," Velina agreed. "I know that he will be very happy with so many animals including, of course, the horse the Marquis has given him."

"He'll be fine with us. So you don't need to worry your head about him, my Lady. We'll make a good home for him and that's what every child needs."

"It certainly is," Velina agreed.

She thanked Mrs. Batley profusely, kissed Johnny, who was still thinking of names for the new puppies, and then went back with Batley to the front of the house.

As she entered the drawing room, she realised that she was now seeing the Marquis as he should look, in full evening dress with a pearl stud on his chest and buttons to match on his waistcoat.

In his satin breeches and silk stockings he looked very different from how Neil Barlow had looked.

For a moment they just gazed at each other.

Then, as they were alone, the Marquis held out his arms and Velina ran towards him.

He kissed her until the whole room seemed to be spinning round.

Then he declared,

"You are lovely, you are adorable and, my darling, the Fairytale has come to its traditional ending."

"Of course it has," Velina whispered. "I love you, I love you, Neil, and we will live happily ever after."

Then the Marquis was kissing her again.

Kissing her until they felt they reached the stars.

They had found the other half of themselves.

They had found the sublime love that comes from God and which Velina had always prayed for.

It was a love that came not only from their hearts but from their souls.

"I love you, I adore you," the Marquis was saying as he kissed her again.

Then he went on kissing her.

And Velina knew that their Divine love, which can only come from God, was all theirs for this life and for all Eternity, for ever and always.